She heard a small cold voice in her head whisper, *So this is seduction.* And knew she was in real danger here.

Because Raf was a master of th̶̶̶̶̶̶̶ come here for her su̶̶̶̶̶̶̶̶̶̶̶̶̶̶̶̶̶̶̶̶ isfied with nothing ̶̶̶̶̶̶̶̶̶̶̶̶̶̶̶̶̶̶̶̶̶̶̶̶ould consider this i̶̶̶̶̶̶̶̶̶̶̶̶̶̶̶̶̶̶̶̶̶̶̶̶̶̶ real contest for hi̶̶̶̶̶̶̶̶̶̶̶̶̶̶̶̶̶̶̶̶̶̶̶ she would be clingi̶̶̶̶̶̶̶̶̶̶̶̶̶̶̶̶̶̶̶̶̶̶̶̶.

Raf allowed his ̶̶̶̶̶̶ ̶̶̶ deepen fractionally, took his mouth from hers for a heartbeat, then kissed her again, running the tip of his tongue delicately along the line of her lips, coaxing them to part for him.

His mouth twisted ruefully and he drew her more closely into his arms.

And for one blind, greedy moment she lost the power of speech, along with the ability to think rationally. Her brain was in free fall, her body startled—pierced by a need she'd never known before or even suspected could exist. She felt him smile against her skin.

'This is our wedding night,' he said softly. 'Here and now. And I will mark it with another promise to you, *mia cara*. I swear that there will come a time—some day, some night soon—when you will desire me as much as I want you now.'

Sara Craven was born in South Devon, and grew up surrounded by books in a house by the sea. After leaving grammar school she worked as a local journalist, covering everything from flower shows to murders. She started writing for Harlequin Mills & Boon in 1975. Sara has appeared as a contestant on the UK Channel Four gameshow *Fifteen to One*, and in 1997 won the title of Television Mastermind of Great Britain.

Sara shares her Somerset home with a West Highland white terrier called Bertie Wooster, several thousand books, and an amazing video and DVD collection.

When she's not writing, she likes to travel in Europe, particularly Greece and Italy. She loves music, theatre, cooking, and eating in good restaurants, but reading will always be her greatest passion.

Since the birth of her twin grandchildren in New York City, she has become a regular visitor to the Big Apple.

Recent titles by the same author:

BRIDE OF DESIRE
WIFE AGAINST HER WILL
THE COUNT'S BLACKMAIL BARGAIN
HIS WEDDING-NIGHT HEIR

THE FORCED
BRIDE

BY
SARA CRAVEN

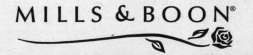

All the characters in this book have no existence outside the imagination of the author, and have no relation whatsoever to anyone bearing the same name or names. They are not even distantly inspired by any individual known or unknown to the author, and all the incidents are pure invention.

First published in Great Britain 2006
Paperback edition 2007
Harlequin Mills & Boon Limited,
Eton House, 18-24 Paradise Road, Richmond, Surrey TW9 1SR

© Sara Craven 2006

ISBN-13: 978 0 263 85294 3
ISBN-10: 0 263 85294 6

Set in Times Roman 10 on 10¾ pt
01-0207-62967

Printed and bound in Spain
by Litografia Rosés, S.A., Barcelona

THE FORCED BRIDE

CHAPTER ONE

'NO,' SAID Emily. She spoke with cool clarity, but her green eyes flashed at the two lawyers on the other side of the desk. 'Not a divorce. You will kindly inform your client that I want an annulment.'

The younger man gasped audibly and received a reproving glance from his senior, Arturo Mazzini, who took off his glasses, wiped them and replaced them on his nose.

'But, Contessa,' he said gently, 'that is surely just—a question of emphasis. The important matter must be the actual dissolution of your marriage, not how it is done.'

His placatory smile was not returned.

'I can decide for myself what is, or is not important,' said Emily. 'A divorce—even the no-fault variety that your client is offering—suggests that a marriage really existed between us. I wish to make it perfectly clear to the world that it has not. That I am not, and never have been, the wife of Count Rafaele Di Salis—in the usual sense of the word,' she added.

Signor Mazzini looked appalled. 'Clear—to the world?' he repeated. 'But you cannot mean that, Contessa. Any arrangement between yourself and the Conte Di Salis must be a private one, its terms not meant to be divulged.'

'I wasn't responsible for the arrangement of my marriage,' Emily told him stonily. 'My father was. Nor did I offer any guarantees about the ending of it. And please don't call me Contessa,' she went on. 'It's hardly appropriate under the circumstances. Miss Blake will be just fine.'

There was an uneasy silence. Signor Mazzini produced a fine linen handkerchief and applied it to his forehead.

'Is it too warm in here, *signore*?' his antagonist asked more kindly. 'Would you like me to open a window?'

Both men repressed a shiver. There had been a sharp frost that morning and the formal gardens around Langborne Manor were still silvered over. Indoors, too, the elderly central heating system left a lot to be desired, although, to Signor Mazzini's certain knowledge, the Conte Di Salis had offered more than once in the past three years to have it replaced.

'You are all goodness,' he returned. 'But no, I thank you.' There was a pause, then he leaned forward. 'Contessa—Miss Blake—I beg you to reconsider. The divorce would be a mere formality and the settlement terms my client proposes are more than generous.'

'I want nothing from the Count.' Emily lifted her chin. 'As soon as I'm twenty one, he will no longer be in control of my affairs. My father's money and this house will finally be mine. I need nothing else.'

She sat back in her chair, the low winter sun slanting in through the long sash window behind her striking fire from her auburn hair.

Young Pietro Celli pretended to busy himself with the papers in the file in front of him while he studied her unobtrusively. Too thin, too pale and altogether too tense, he thought, recalling with renewed appreciation the frankly sinuous curves of the Count's latest mistress, which he had been permitted to admire on a number of occasions—although only from a discreet distance.

The slim hands were bare, he noticed, so heaven only knew what the Count's soon-to-be-ex-wife had done with His Excellency's wedding ring, or the Di Salis sapphire, which would have to be returned, of course, however the marriage reached its end.

But her eyes—Madonna *mia*!—they were amazing—the colour of emeralds, and with those long lashes too. However, the rest of the face—nondescript, he decided with a mental shrug.

And clearly a virago along with all her other faults. Small wonder, then, if a connoisseur of women like Rafaele Di Salis had opted for a marriage in name only. Who could blame him?

'Unless, of course, your client has gambled my entire inheri-

tance away on some dodgy financial deal,' this impossible young
woman was adding lightly. 'Perhaps you've been sent here to
break the bad news.'

Signor Mazzini bristled, while Pietro felt his jaw drop and had
to hastily recover himself.

'That is a most damaging allegation, *signorina*,' the older
man said at last, his voice icy. 'Your husband has dealt with the
trust in an exemplary manner, have no doubt of that. You will be
a wealthy young woman.' Much wealthier than you deserve, the
note in his voice suggested.

Emily sighed. 'I wasn't serious. I'm perfectly aware that
Count Di Salis is one of the stars of the world of finance.' She
added stiltedly, 'And, naturally, I'm grateful for anything he's
been able to do on my behalf.'

The lawyer spread his hands, almost helplessly. 'Then, if I
may be permitted to ask, why not show your gratitude by
acceding to the plan for a divorce?'

Emily pushed her chair back and rose. She walked over to the
window and stood looking out. Her slender figure was clad in a
cream woollen shirt tucked into close-fitting black cord trousers,
with a wide leather belt reducing her waist to a handspan. The
rich glow of her hair was drawn back to the nape of her neck and
fastened with a black ribbon bow.

She said quietly, 'Because, when I remarry, I wish the ceremony
to be held in our parish church, but the vicar is a strong tradition-
alist and won't agree if I'm divorced. I also intend to wear white for
the occasion so that my bridegroom will know that he isn't getting
damaged goods.' She paused. 'Is that plain enough for your client?'

'But your present marriage is still a fact, Miss Blake.' Signor
Mazzini's reminder was brusque. 'Is it not a little soon to be
planning another wedding?'

'There is no marriage,' Emily said. 'Just a business deal
nearing the end of its shelf life. And I can hardly be bound by
that when considering my—future.'

She turned back. 'Now may I offer you both some tea?' Her
polite smile did not reach her eyes. 'I'm afraid the coffee in this
house would hardly appeal to you.'

Signor Mazzini rose. 'I thank you, but no. I think we both need a little space—to consider. Perhaps we may have a further discussion tomorrow, *signorina*, in the hope you may have decided to—think again. Because, I tell you plainly, His Excellency will not agree to an annulment.'

'But why not?' The emerald eyes opened wide. 'He must want to be rid of me, as much as I want my own freedom. And, anyway, I deserve some reward for three years of dutiful boredom,' she added, shrugging. 'I've acted as his hostess here and in London when required, and turned a blind eye to his notoriously public private life. A steep learning curve if ever there was one.' Her tone stung. 'Now he can oblige me for a change.'

'In your English history, *signorina*, you have a custom, I think, of throwing down the gauntlet.' Signor Mazzini's tone held a touch of grimness. 'In this case, such a challenge to His Excellency would not be wise.'

Emily's laugh held a hard note. 'Oh, dear, have I insulted Count Rafaele's machismo? Dented his reputation by suggesting that there's at least one woman in the known world who doesn't find him irresistible—and that's his alleged wife?' She shrugged. 'Well, any damage to his male pride is—just unfortunate, because I have no intention of changing my mind. Please make that—ultra-clear to your client.'

She moved to the fireplace, where a log fire was smouldering, and rang the bell beside the mantelpiece.

'Also suggest to him that we begin proceedings to end the marriage without delay,' she added crisply. 'After all, my twenty-first birthday's in three months' time and I would really like to be single again by then.'

'I will convey your wishes to His Excellency,' Signor Mazzini said with a small stiff bow. Or, at least, a carefully edited version of them, he amended silently as the housekeeper arrived to show them out.

When she was alone, Emily dropped limply into the big leather armchair that stood to the left of the wide hearth. She'd presented a bold front to her visitors and only she knew that her stomach had been churning and her legs trembling under her throughout the interview.

But it was done and she'd taken her first shaky steps towards freedom. And now her visitors would be on their way back to Rome or New York—or wherever Raf happened to be at present—with the bad news.

If that was what it was, she thought defensively. Why should he care about one less notch on his bedpost among so many?

She curled up in the big wing-chair that had once belonged to her father and closed her eyes.

Oh, Dad, she whispered forlornly. You did me no favours at all when you pushed me into this farce of a marriage.

I should never—never have agreed to it, but what else could I do when you were so ill and made me promise?

But at least it's not a life sentence. Raf's keeping his word about that.

On the other hand, she reminded herself defensively, he's doing me no favours either. He only agreed to marry me because he was in debt to my father and this was a way of paying it off.

Because I was certainly the last bride he'd ever have considered in ordinary circumstances.

Not that I cared at the time what he thought or what he wanted. Not when I was so miserable about Simon. When I really thought he'd gone for good.

At the time I felt so lonely and humiliated that if Count Dracula had proposed I'd probably have accepted him.

Not, she told herself, lips tightening, that Raf had any vampire qualities. He was more on the lines of a black panther, roaming the financial jungles to seek his prey. And how he'd ever become involved with her father was one of life's great mysteries.

Emily had first become aware of him when she was seventeen and had just arrived home from school for the Christmas holidays.

She'd come flying into the house as usual, leaving the chauffeur to follow with her luggage, and gone straight to her father's study, flinging the door wide with an exuberant, 'Pops, darling, I'm home,' only to find herself confronted by a tall young man, someone she'd never seen before, rising politely from his chair at her entrance.

She halted instantly, lips parting in surprise and embarrassment, her astonished gaze registering a confused but vivid impression of black, curling hair, tawny skin and lambent hazel eyes flecked with green and gold that, she realised, were studying her closely in return. And, at the same moment, she saw the firm mouth quirk as if some sudden thought had amused him.

She felt herself bristle instinctively and said quickly, stammering a little, 'Dad, I'm sorry. I didn't realise you were engaged with anyone.'

'It's fine, my dear. I'm sure Count di Salis will forgive your unceremonious arrival.' Her father was smiling as he came round the desk to take her hands and kiss her, but his greeting seemed faintly muted and he didn't sweep her up into the accustomed bear hug. 'Isn't that so, Rafaele?'

'It was a charming interruption.' The newcomer's voice was low and resonant, his English flawless. He stepped forward, taking the hand she had awkwardly proffered. 'So this is your Emilia, *signore.*'

His touch was light, but she felt a sudden jolt of awareness, as unexpected as it was unfamiliar. It was like receiving a minor electric shock, she thought, unnerved, and wanted to snatch her fingers from his clasp, at the same time telling him her name was plain 'Emily' and not some Italianised version of it which somehow made it personal to him. A notion she found oddly disturbing.

And in the same instant found her hand released, as if the Count had sensed her inner withdrawal and reacted to it instantly.

He said with perfect courtesy, 'It is my pleasure to meet you, *signorina,*' then looked across at Sir Travers Blake. 'You are a fortunate man, my friend.'

'I think so too.' Her father's hand rested momentarily on her shoulder. 'Now, run along and get your unpacking sorted, my pet,' he added quietly. 'And we'll join you for tea later.'

Normally, Emily thought, as she looked back, if Dad had been busy when I arrived home, I'd have kicked off my shoes and curled up in this very chair waiting for him to finish. Yet somehow I knew, even then, that I wasn't going to be allowed to say a proper 'hello' and that everything was in the process of changing.

What I didn't bargain for was the extent of that change.

When she'd reluctantly emerged into the hall again, she'd found Mrs Penistone, the housekeeper, hovering and looking anxious.

'Oh, Miss Emily, I was supposed to tell you that your father couldn't be disturbed,' she said apologetically. 'I hope he isn't cross.'

'He didn't seem to be.' Emily swooped on her last remaining bag and started up the stairs. 'Don't worry about it, Penny dear. We're all having tea together later, so I guess I'm forgiven for blundering in. And I'll apologise again when his visitor has gone.'

'Oh, but he's not going,' Mrs Penistone informed her. 'He's staying for Christmas. Your father told me yesterday to prepare the Gold Room for him.'

'He did?' The news stopped Emily in her tracks. 'But he never has guests to stay at Christmas. He's always said peace on earth should start right here at home. He only gives the Boxing Day party on sufferance to the selected few.'

'Well, not this year, Miss Emily.' The older woman pursed her lips. 'He's invited everyone in the neighbourhood.'

'Even the Aubreys from High Gables?' Emily tried to sound casual. 'Goodness, he is pushing the boat out.'

He must really want to impress Count Whatsit, she thought as she went into her room. But if that meant Simon Aubrey was coming to their party, then she could almost be grateful to this unexpected intruder.

My gorgeous, wonderful Simon, she whispered silently, and smiled as she began to conjure up his image in her mind. But the picture that presented itself was a very different one. Not Simon's boyish good looks at all, but an older, darker face that watched her with a faint smile. A face that, while intrinsically and powerfully masculine with its taut lines, high cheekbones and aquiline nose, managed at the same time to be—somehow— beautiful.

And she found herself suddenly remembering her art teacher describing the subject of some Renaissance painting as looking like 'one of the fallen angels' .

Now I know exactly what she meant, Emily thought. Because there was no hint of softness about this Rafaele Di Salis. On the contrary, there was an uncompromising toughness about his mouth and jaw and a cool arrogance in his glance that seemed to tell the world to beware. And she found herself giving a faint shiver.

As she unpacked, she made specific plans about what she

would do if she ever discovered the Count di Salis was watching her again. Not that it was likely, she hastily assured herself.

But if—if it happened, then she would stare back, coolly and calmly, but, at the same time, with enough hauteur to make him realise his scrutiny was totally unwelcome and remember his good manners.

But she soon discovered that this careful planning was all in vain. Because it soon became apparent that, as far as the Count was concerned, she might as well have been invisible. And, on the few occasions when he seemed to notice her, he treated her with a distant politeness that chilled her with its formality—a reluctant adult dealing with a child, she thought, seething.

To make matters worse, her father seemed unusually preoccupied. In fact, she hardly saw anything of him because he seemed closeted in his study with Count Di Salis for hours at a time.

This wasn't the normal run-up to Christmas by any means, Emily thought wistfully, although she'd told herself repeatedly that she was just being silly and selfish. That her father had a perfect right to invite anyone he wanted to his own house, at any time of the year.

But she'd grown accustomed, since her mother's death five years before, to having him all to herself during the school holidays, and she wished that the Count di Salis had paid his visit at some other time.

As it was, she was beginning to feel as if she was, in fact, the interloper here. That her presence was an obstacle to all these ongoing discussions.

She told herself that there must be some big deal brewing, but she knew better than to ask and did her best not to feel resentful.

Sir Travers had never discussed the ramifications of his property development empire with her, invariably telling her she was too young to understand. However, she was sure in her own mind that it would have been different if she'd been a boy. That her training as his successor would already have begun in earnest.

But he'd made it equally apparent, kindly but firmly, that his only daughter would have no role to play in the future running of the company.

Daddy the Dinosaur, she thought with a small sigh.

Instead, with his total approval, she'd been nudged by her teachers into studying Fine Arts at university. And while she wasn't opposed to the idea, she wasn't ecstatic in her enthusiasm either.

On the other hand, now Simon was in her life, her future might take a very different path, she thought, as glowing excitement rose inside her.

The Aubreys and the Blakes had never been on particularly close terms, and while Simon, who was Mr Aubrey's nephew, had been a frequent visitor in the past, he'd not taken much notice of Emily until the previous summer, when she'd been asked over to High Gables one glorious Sunday afternoon to play tennis on the new all-weather court they'd just had installed.

The invitation had come from Jilly, the Aubreys' only daughter, a cool, leggy blonde, three years older than Emily, who'd made it languidly clear that she was only being asked to make up the numbers, because someone else had dropped out at the last minute.

It had been an unpromising beginning, but when Simon had smiled at her and claimed her as his partner, offering a charming apology in advance for being rusty, Emily had felt much better. And when they'd won, she'd found herself basking in his admiration.

After that, Simon had made sure that she was invited over nearly every day to play tennis or swim in the Aubreys' pool, although Jilly had not been best pleased by this turn of events and had made no effort to hide it.

But Emily told herself that Jilly's quiet malice didn't matter. Because she was falling in love and she didn't care who knew it.

And—heaven of heavens—Simon seemed to feel the same. Everything he said to her—each time he took her in his arms— was a promise for the future.

Naturally, there could be no formal acknowledgement of their relationship for at least another year, and both of them had recognised this and discussed it.

For one thing, she had to coax her father into becoming firstly accustomed and then receptive to the idea. And this, she knew, would be no simple matter, especially as Simon was between jobs and editorial positions on magazines did not appear to be easy to find.

'I don't want to go to him cap in hand,' Simon had told her

ruefully on more than one occasion. 'Especially as I get the impression no one is ever going to be good enough for his lovely girl.'

Emily had to, reluctantly, agree. But she consoled herself with the certainty that once her father got to know Simon properly he would like him. And the Boxing Day party would be an ideal opportunity for them to begin their closer acquaintance. She was sure of that too.

But first she had to negotiate Christmas Day, which was easier than expected because her father, as if aware he'd been neglecting her, made a determined effort to be the affectionate and jovial companion she was used to.

There was one tricky moment, however, when she was thrown completely by Rafaele Di Salis thanking her politely for the book on local history she'd apparently given him. Knowing full well that she'd neglected to buy him anything at all, and that this was her father's doing, Emily stammered an awkward response, blushing vividly under his ironic gaze.

He himself had presented her with a dozen exquisite handkerchieves, trimmed with handmade Italian lace.

Correct and so—bo-ring, Emily decided. A duty present if ever there was one, which made her feel slightly better about the book.

But she was grateful when he absented himself during the afternoon to go for a long walk, leaving her alone with her father to play backgammon, an annual needle-match with no quarter given, or expected.

'So what do you think of Rafaele?' her father asked suddenly as she set up the board for the game.

She shrugged. 'I try not to think about him at all,' she returned nonchalantly, reaching for the dice box.

For a moment she thought her father had frowned, but decided he was simply wearing his deep-concentration expression in honour of the event's solemnity.

'You've improved,' he announced later as Mrs Penistone came in to draw the curtains and bring the tea.

Emily pulled a face at him. 'You let me win,' she accused as she put the board and counters back in their leather case.

'Nonsense,' he said robustly and got up to poke the fire.

The moment his back was turned, she became aware that

the housekeeper was beckoning to her, and she followed her from the room.

'Is something wrong?'

'There's been a special delivery for you, Miss Emily—at the back door.'

Mrs Penistone was looking roguish. 'Brought by a nice young man.'

'Oh.' Emily coloured as the older woman produced a small flat package tied up in Christmas wrap. It had to be from Simon, she thought, her heart beating faster, so she would take it to her room and open it in private.

On her way along the gallery upstairs, she took the tiny card from its envelope and read the scrawled message. 'For Emily— my fantasy girl. S.'

Unable to control her curiosity any longer, she tore away the wrapping and paused, staring down at what lay in the folds of paper.

It was underwear, she realised, but not like anything she had ever worn in her life. There was a bra consisting of two triangles of filmy black gauze joined by narrow ribbon and a matching thong.

For a moment she felt confused. So far, Simon's courtship of her had been deliberately restrained, even though there were times when his slow kisses made her ache with frustration. He'd always said he was prepared to be patient—that she was worth waiting for.

Until now. Until this—astonishing *volte face*. Was this— really—how Simon thought of her? she wondered, her skin warming. How he saw her? And if so...

'Emilia.'

She hadn't heard the door of the Gold Room open, let alone the sound of his approach, yet there was Rafaele Di Salis, standing right in front of her. And, jolted out of her reverie, she started violently, her slackened grasp allowing the tiny scraps of lingerie and the accompanying card to fall to the carpet between them.

For a moment, Emily stood, stricken. Oh, God, she moaned under her breath, diving frantically to retrieve them. But Rafaele Di Salis was there before her, straightening with the bra and thong dangling incongruously from a fastidious forefinger.

His brows lifted. 'A gift from an admirer?' His tone was coolly dispassionate.

'I don't think that's any of your business,' she returned curtly. If she'd blushed before, she was burning now from head to foot. *Oh, why hadn't she waited until she was safely in her room to open her parcel? For him, of all men, to see Simon's present.* 'May I have them back, please?'

'*Certamente.*' He dropped them back into their wrappings with an almost disdainful flick of the hand.

Emily bit her lip. All she really wanted to do now was walk away from him and die in a place where her corpse would never be discovered. On the other hand, she didn't want her father to receive a full description of the incident, she realised resignedly. So—something would have to be done.

She said stiltedly, 'I—I thought you were out walking.'

He shrugged. 'Your father suggested I return in time for tea. He said it was quite an occasion.' He glanced down at the bra and thong, his mouth twisting. 'I see he was right.'

'They were intended as a joke,' she said quickly. 'But I don't think Daddy would find it very funny.'

'Then, perhaps, we should not distress him by mentioning it.'

'No,' she said. Adding reluctantly, 'Thank you.'

She waited, but he made no attempt to move, and she was aware of his gaze resting on her reflectively.

She cleared her throat. 'I—I know what you must be thinking…'

'No,' he said quite gently. 'You do not.' And handed her the card with Simon's message. 'As a matter of fact, I too am enjoying a fantasy,' he went on. 'But mine does not involve clothing—of any kind.'

He gave her a cool, impersonal smile and walked on, leaving Emily gasping as if she'd been winded.

She spent a long time in her room, trying to summon up the courage to go down and face the tiny sandwiches, the feather-light scones with cream and the huge elaborate Christmas cake that Mrs Penistone had provided. Because she'd be expected to sample all of them under the sardonic gaze of their guest, and any loss of appetite would be noted and commented on by her father.

Which, in turn, would provide further opportunities for that appalling—that *vile* Rafaele Di Salis to amuse himself at her expense, she realised stormily.

Because that was all it had been. Yet another dubious joke, but one which he'd had no right to make.

Except that a girl who'd just received a secret gift of suggestive underwear from her boyfriend could hardly be prim about some mild sexual teasing. But, however she rationalised it, the memory still made her squirm uncomfortably.

I just wish he'd complete his business with Daddy and go, she told herself as she put the underwear back in its wrappings and buried it deep in a drawer, then went slowly and reluctantly down to the drawing room.

'Well?' Simon breathed into her ear. 'Are you wearing them?'

Emily looked down at herself—at the demure white silk shirt with its deep Puritan-style collar, and the ankle-length velvet skirt in shades of dark blue and turquoise.

'Er—no.' She made her tone placatory. 'They didn't seem quite right—not under this.'

'Well, maybe,' he conceded moodily. 'Tell me something, Em. Don't you ever get tired of playing Daddy's little girl? You're past the age of consent, so isn't it time you grew up and started being a woman? My woman, in fact?'

She gasped. 'I thought we'd agreed to wait.'

'And I've been waiting, for God's sake. Have a heart, honey. I'm only human and I'm getting sick of walking away from you with just an ache in my guts.'

Her cheeks warmed and she looked round in embarrassment. 'Simon—keep your voice down. People will hear you.'

'What are they going to hear? That I want you? That'll come as no surprise to anyone in the neighbourhood—except your father, maybe.' He moved fractionally closer. 'Isn't there some way we can be together, sweetheart?'

'You mean this evening?' Emily was incredulous. 'But I'm my father's hostess. I can't just—disappear. Besides, I'm under orders to make sure that our house guest meets everyone,' she added with a touch of bitterness.

'You mean the tall Mediterranean job who's been roaming round the village lately?' Simon snorted. 'I wouldn't worry about *him*.'

'But I have to worry. I was in trouble yesterday for spending time in my room when I should have been dancing attendance on him. Daddy actually ticked me off about it, when I was on my way up to bed.'

She sighed. 'So now I'm supposed to compensate for yesterday's rudeness by looking after him tonight. Making sure he's not bored—keeping his drink freshened and all that stuff.'

'You could have a problem there,' Simon informed her. 'Because all the women in the room are clustered round him, drooling. You'd probably have to kill to reach him.' His voice sank to a persuasive whisper. 'Sweetheart, this is a big house. There must be somewhere we can go—just for a while?'

Emily bit her lip. Was that how he wanted their first time together? she asked herself, troubled. A snatched encounter in some empty bedroom with the threat of discovery hanging over them?

She said quietly, 'Simon, I can't. My father's bound to miss me and we can't take the risk.'

'Later, then. When the party's over and everyone's gone.' His voice was urgent. 'I'll give it a couple of hours, then I'll come back across the garden, so leave the conservatory unlocked for me, hmm?'

He paused. 'Please, darling. It would mean so much to know you're ready to trust yourself to me.'

Emily hesitated miserably, then nodded. 'If—that's what you want.'

His grin was triumphant. 'Oh, you'll want it too, my pet, I promise you that. And wear my present, eh?'

Emily moved away, aware that her mouth was dry and her heart thudding uncomfortably. Some instinct made her look across the room and she realised that, hemmed in as he was, Rafaele Di Salis was watching her, his dark face expressionless.

And she'd already turned away before she remembered she'd intended to stare back.

She was on edge for the rest of the evening. Someone—some stranger outside herself—moved through the groups of people, smiling and talking, but was unable to recollect a single word that had been said.

However there was nothing wrong with her eyesight. And it seemed that Simon had been perfectly correct about Rafaele Di Salis's ability to attract the women in the room. In particular, Jilly Aubrey seemed so attached to his side that it would probably need a surgical operation to remove her. Which proved, Emily told herself waspishly, that there was no accounting for taste.

It seemed to have been a good party, however. Everyone was saying so as they reluctantly departed. In the hallway, someone produced a sprig of mistletoe and kisses were freely exchanged amid laughter and cheering. Emily had to submit to her fair share, smiling with spurious brightness as she did so. But Simon was not among the claimants.

'I didn't see the Aubreys leave.' She tried to speak casually as the door closed behind their last guests.

'They went nearly an hour ago,' Sir Travers returned. 'Apart from the girl Jillian,' he added disapprovingly. 'She stayed on, having persuaded to Rafaele to drive her home later.'

Now why does that not surprise me? Emily thought ironically.

The clearing up after the party was accomplished swiftly and efficiently by Mrs Penistone and the extra staff hired for the evening, and eventually Emily was able to go up to her room, but not before she'd slipped unobtrusively through the dining room to the conservatory beyond and unlocked the door.

She could only hope that the housekeeper would not decide to carry out a last-minute double-check.

Or was that really what she was hoping for? Because, if she was honest, she felt almost sick with apprehension as she undressed and took a quick shower.

Reluctantly, she put on the bra and thong and took a wincing look at herself in the mirror. She didn't look or feel in the least sexy, she thought wretchedly. Just uncomfortable and—incredibly stupid. But if this was how Simon wanted her…

All the same, she was glad to cover up by zipping herself into her dark green velour robe.

Why was she hesitating? she wondered, as she brushed her hair into a silken cloud on her shoulders. Tonight was a turning point in her life—the magic time when she would belong at last to Simon—the man she loved—and it would be beautiful—wonderful, because he would make it so for her.

And, drawing a deep breath, she slipped out of her room, closing the door behind her with immense care, and went silently down the shadowed stairs to keep her rendezvous.

CHAPTER TWO

EVEN now, three years later, Emily could remember every detail of that short journey. Could recall the brush of the stair carpet under her bare feet, the way the shadows had seemed to distort even the most familiar objects and the soft creaking and groaning as the old house settled for the night.

With every step she'd expected lights to blaze on and her father's voice demanding to know what she was doing.

She supposed she'd have to say that she couldn't sleep and was going to the kitchen to heat some milk. He'd believe her, because she'd never given him cause to do otherwise. Or not until now, she'd thought, her throat closing.

More than once she'd been tempted to turn back. To take refuge in her room and find some excuse that would placate Simon for her failure to show.

But I love him, she'd reminded herself almost feverishly. I should be wanting to make him happy, not pacify him.

When she was in his arms, she would feel differently. She was sure of it. Convinced that this little knot of coldness in the pit of her stomach would dissolve into something altogether warmer and more receptive.

And yet...

She'd have been lying to herself if she hadn't hoped that her first time with Simon would have been more *meaningful* in some way. More romantic than these hasty and covert moments ahead of her.

Although, as she'd gathered from the conversation of her more sophisticated school friends, usually the first time was no big deal. Merely something that needed to be got out of the way, so that more pleasurable experiences could follow.

There was also the vexed question of birth control. Emily reckoned uneasily that she was the only girl in the sixth form not to be on the pill. But would Simon have guessed this and made his own arrangements, or would she have to pretend everything was all right—and risk the consequences?

She swallowed past the tightness in her throat. Her father would be angry and disappointed with her, of course, but as she and Simon were planning to be married anyway, would it really be so awful if the wedding date had to be moved forward because she was pregnant?

Well, the short answer to that was yes. Because it was the last thing she wanted to happen.

The situation would be much easier to handle if Simon's career wasn't currently on hold, she thought forlornly. How could he cope with a wife and baby without a regular salary or a home of his own?

Her father might offer him something, she supposed, but she wouldn't count on it. Not if he had Simon foisted on him as a son-in-law before they'd even had a chance to become properly acquainted, let alone friends.

Taking a deep breath, she opened the door to the conservatory and slipped inside like a small, quiet ghost.

It was one of her favourite places in the house, its warmth like a blanket, enveloping her in comfort. She stood still for a moment, eyes closed, breathing the raw earthy smells and listening to the familiar muted hum of the heating system.

There was no other sound. No movement either. And Emily realised with something very like relief that Simon wasn't there.

But perhaps she should allow him a few minutes' grace, she thought reluctantly. After all, she couldn't go to bed leaving the outside door unsecured, yet she certainly didn't want him arriving late either, rattling at the lock and wakening the entire household in a frustrated attempt to gain access.

Oh God, I should never—never—have agreed to any of this, she groaned inwardly, sinking down on a bench next to the miniature palms and peering at the face of her watch in the gloom. I'm not the stuff conspirators are made of.

She sat tensely, hands clasped in her lap, willing the moments to pass more quickly.

When she saw Simon next, she would pretend it had never happened, she told herself. She'd tell him her father had been on the prowl, and she hadn't dared leave her room. Hope that he hadn't had a wasted journey.

She was just getting to her feet when she realised that the door to the garden was opening silently to admit the dark figure of a man.

For a brief second she froze in the realisation that it was too late to slip away.

This is Simon, she reminded herself urgently. This is the man you love and want. And it's time to commit yourself to that love, once and for always.

She drew a breath, then went to him, running, flinging herself into the arms that instantly closed about her as she lifted her face for his kiss.

But, instead of the passionate demand she'd expected, he was almost restrained, keeping his ardour well in check, and Emily was grateful for it.

Eyes shut, she gave herself up to the pleasure of the cool, gentle brush of his lips against hers, his exploration of the soft contours of her mouth as if this was strange, uncharted territory to him.

As if…

And in that same moment, she knew with total clarity that this was wrong—all wrong. That the hard male body she'd pressed herself against so ardently was taller, leaner than Simon's, and altogether more muscular. That she was not being held and kissed as Simon held and kissed her. And that this man even smelled differently, Simon's familiar brand of aftershave having been replaced by something infinitely more subtle and expensive.

But only too recognisable, just the same…

Oh, God, she whimpered in silent horror, as realisation dawned. Oh, God, it's—him.

Gasping, she tore her lips from his and pushed at him violently.

'Let go of me.' Her voice was shaking. 'Let go of me at once, damn you.'

'You mean this entrancing welcome is not intended for me, after all?' Rafaele Di Salis asked mockingly. 'I am desolate.'

But he relaxed his clasp sufficiently for Emily to take an uneven step backwards, out of range. At the same time, he clicked the switch by the door and the overhead light went on, catching her in the act of scrubbing violently at her mouth with her hand in an attempt to remove any lingering traces of his kiss.

To cover her confusion, Emily went into attack mode. 'What do you think you're doing—creeping into the place like a burglar?'

His brows lifted sardonically. 'Are you saying that you mistook me for a thief—and not Simon Aubrey?'

'Simon,' she said curtly, 'need not concern you.'

'Ah, but he does, Emilia. Because I fear that he will not be able to keep his appointment with you tonight, after all.'

She stiffened. 'He told—you that?'

'No.' Rafaele Di Salis shrugged. 'I told him so, when I encountered him in the garden a short while ago.'

She gasped. 'You were spying on us?'

'I had just returned from driving Signorina Aubrey home and heard him crashing through the shrubbery as I walked back to the house. He is fortunate there are no dogs on the premises, or he would have woken the whole household—including your father.' He allowed a significant pause. 'I persuaded him that his visit was—inappropriate and he left.'

She said chokingly, 'And what gives you the right to interfere in my affairs?'

'You mean there have been others?' He tutted. 'And I would have sworn that Simon Aubrey was the first.' He glanced round. 'And I must tell you, *cara*, that this is hardly the most comfortable setting for so momentous an event as losing your virginity.'

For a long moment Emily was incapable of speech, aware that every inch of her skin was burning with embarrassment.

At last she said hoarsely, 'You are—disgusting.'

He laughed. 'No, merely practical. Besides, your would-be lover seemed in no mood for a tender seduction when I met him just now. Frankly, he appeared ill-tempered. And, when I arrived at his uncle's house earlier, it was clear there had been a family disagreement of some magnitude in which he was involved.'

'That is none of your business!'

'I agree,' Rafaele told her cordially. 'Which is why I made an excuse and left at once, without the coffee I had been promised.'

She glared at him. 'Or anything else, presumably. Is that why you decided to ruin my time with Simon, *signore*—because you'd missed out with Jilly?'

He said gently, 'That, *mia cara*, is a vulgarity not worthy of you.' He paused. 'I look on your father as my friend, Emilia, and I would try to prevent anything that would distress him. And the discovery that you had agreed to a secret liaison under his own roof would be a serious blow to him. You must know that. Your young man should have more regard for your honour.'

Emily flung back her head. 'It so happens, *signore*, that Simon and I are engaged to be married. We were meeting tonight to—to discuss our plans for the future, and not for the sordid reason you imagine.'

His stride towards her was so quick and purposeful that she didn't have a chance to step backwards. And, before she could defend herself, his hand had snaked out and pulled down the zip on her robe almost to the waist. The edges fell apart, revealing to his gaze the flimsy black triangles that barely concealed her nipples.

He said contemptuously, 'It seems I am not the only one with a sordid imagination, *signorina*. Let me tell you that you are too young and far too lovely to require such tawdry adornment. You disappoint me.'

'How dare you?' Her voice was a strangled croak as she struggled to cover herself again, her fingers made clumsy by haste and shame. 'Oh, God, how dare you—touch me? Insult me? You call yourself Daddy's friend? He'll throw you out of the house when I tell him…'

'When you tell him—precisely what?' Rafaele Di Salis cut impatiently across her stumbling words. 'What you were doing here? Why you were dressed as you are?' He shook his head. 'No, Emilia, I recommend that you hold your peace about tonight, as I shall. Now, go to your room,' he added almost wearily. 'And I will lock up here.'

She did not wait to argue, but fled. In the quiet of her room, she threw herself across the bed, burying her face in the covers, as shock and misery overwhelmed her.

I want to die, she told herself passionately, a sob rising in her throat. Just to die. Because then I'll never have to see Rafaele Di Salis again.

But, for the time being, she had to go on living—enduring the terrible memory of his condemnatory gaze and the harsh dismissal of his words.

And, somewhere among all of that, was the realisation that Simon had tamely given up and gone home, which, she discovered wretchedly, didn't seem nearly as bad.

She spent a miserable and restless night, with the covers pulled over her head, and it was a pale, hollow-eyed Emily who went reluctantly down to breakfast the next morning to confront her tormentor the best she could. She'd rehearsed a number of dignified and cutting speeches in case he should make some ill-chosen reference to the night's events, but they proved unnecessary.

Because he wasn't there, and when she forced herself to ask her father about their guest's non-appearance, she was breezily informed that Rafaele Di Salis had left first thing that morning to catch a flight to New York.

'Isn't that rather sudden?' She managed to pour her coffee with a reasonably steady hand.

Sir Travers looked surprised. 'No, my dear. Raf always planned to leave immediately after Boxing Day. Didn't I mention that?'

'Actually, no,' said Emily.

'Well, he's gone, anyway.' Her father paused, then smiled. 'And he asked me to pass on his good wishes for your future happiness.'

'How kind,' Emily said woodenly, and applied herself to her scrambled eggs.

Strange, Emily thought, shifting uneasily in the big chair, that even after the passage of three years, she should have this—instant recall, as if it had all happened yesterday. But maybe unpleasant memories stayed longer in the mind than the cheerful variety.

Not that there'd ever been any really joyous moments to glean from any part of her strange relationship with Raf Di Salis.

The celebration would come when he signed the papers to set her free. And allow her, at last, to marry her first love and put all the pain of separation and misunderstanding behind them.

Her mouth tightened as she remembered how, in the aftermath of that disastrous night, she'd waited in mounting desperation to hear from Simon. But forty-eight endless hours had passed without a word and, as the time lengthened, her pride would not allow her to contact him and demand to know what the hell was going on.

She'd been in the village, parking her bicycle outside the general stores, when Jilly Aubrey had emerged.

'Well, hi,' she drawled, giving Emily the usual disparaging once-over. 'Where's that gorgeous Italian who was staying with you? I want to invite him to our New Year bash, if he's going to be around.'

Emily gave her a cool look. 'I'm afraid you'll be disappointed. He's gone, and he won't be coming back for New Year, or any other time.' *If my prayers are answered…*

Jilly shrugged. 'Don't sound so pleased, honey, because you're in the same boat. Simon's staying on in London, according to Mother.'

'London,' Emily repeated before she could stop herself.

'You mean you don't know?' Jilly's eyes glinted with malice. She lowered her voice confidentially. 'Dad found out over Christmas that he'd been borrowing money from Ma again, and there was a massive explosion, *chez nous*. Fall-out everywhere, my dear. So pretty Cousin Simon's been sent off to seek his fortune, or find a job that will enable him to pay a few of his debts, anyway. If such a thing exists,' she added with a faint sneer. 'Whatever, he won't be allowed back until he's gainfully employed, so I'd look around for another boyfriend if I were you.'

'But I'm not you,' Emily said quietly. 'I believe in Simon and I'm prepared to wait.'

The other girl shrugged again. 'More fool you,' she retorted. 'Don't say you weren't warned.' And she walked down the street to her car and drove away.

Simon could have told me, Emily thought forlornly as she queued for her stamps at the post office counter. In fact, he *should* have told me.

And we didn't even get the chance to say goodbye because of that bloody Rafaele Di Salis.

Even the slightest mention of his name seemed to have the

power to make her burn with rage and humiliation, although she'd done her damnedest to put him out of her mind.

But she was still haunted by the way he'd looked at her that awful night, and it was galling beyond belief that he should be the first man to see her even semi-naked.

One of her first acts after his departure had been to wrap that horrible underwear in newspaper and add it to the incinerator in the garden where the last of the dead leaves were burning.

Gone, she'd told herself. Over and done with. Only, somehow, it didn't seem to be that simple, and she didn't know why.

She tried to give her thoughts a more positive turn as she cycled back to the house, telling herself that it was a good thing that Simon was looking for work—the first step towards the future they were planning. Although it didn't mean, of course, that her father would fall over himself to give them his blessing. But it was a start.

And as for Jilly's remarks—well, Emily decided, she shouldn't give them credence. Simon's cousin had been spiteful over their relationship from the start. And her disappointment over Raf Di Salis hadn't sweetened her disposition either.

Over dinner that evening, she said, 'We aren't having visitors for New Year, by any chance, are we?'

'No one. Why, is there someone you wish to invite?' her father asked.

'No,' Emily said too vehemently. 'Absolutely not. I was just— checking, that's all.'

Sir Travers examined the wine in his glass. 'Did you hope, perhaps, that Rafaele might be joining us?'

'On the contrary,' Emily denied quickly.

He gave her a long, steady look. 'Why do you dislike him?'

'Does there have to be a reason?' Her tone was defensive.

'I suppose not,' he said. 'But I would prefer it if you were friends.' There was a quiet, almost stern note in his voice that Emily knew of old. 'I expect him to be a regular guest here, and as his hostess, my dear, you will make him welcome.'

Emily's heart sank, but she managed a neutral, 'Yes, of course.'

At the same, she surreptitiously crossed her fingers that there would be no return visit from the Count until she was safely back at school.

And it seemed her luck was in, because Raf Di Salis continued to stay away and Emily found the latter part of her holiday truly enjoyable, in spite of Simon's absence.

She was packing to return to school when she eventually heard from him. Simon was back at High Gables just to collect his things, having found work with an import/export company in the City.

Over a snatched lunch at the village pub, Simon explained that, although he was starting at the lowest level, the job could be a stepping stone to real money.

'And I could travel,' he told her exultantly. 'The company has branches all over the world.' He paused, then put his hand over hers. 'And in a few months I'll be earning enough to come back for you.'

Emily smiled and tried to be thrilled for him, but there was a bleakness in her heart that she could not explain. It occurred to her that his words had a hint of afterthought about them. That maybe if he hadn't had belongings to collect from his uncle's house, she might not have heard from him at all.

Also, there seemed to be a tacit agreement between them not to mention the Boxing Night party, and although she was prepared to accept this, she still felt she deserved an explanation, if not an apology.

After all, Simon must know that he wasn't the only one to suffer the embarrassment of an encounter with Raf Di Salis that night. Wasn't he even curious?

But she swiftly told herself she was being unfair. His life was undergoing some sweeping changes, and part of the reason he was undertaking them was for her.

She watched him drive away, clinging to his promise to call her every weekend.

He will come back to me, she whispered to herself, as she waved to him. He will come back. I—I know it.

But clearly not immediately, because he was far too busy. And gradually the phone calls crammed with news of his successes at work, and the friends he was making, began to dwindle away until they stopped completely.

At Easter there was no sign of him, and Emily, hurt and bewildered, could not bring herself to ask for news when she met any of the Aubreys. And, a week or so later, she was completely devastated when the announcement of his engagement to a girl called Rebecca West appeared in *The Times*.

'He's done well for himself,' her father commented curtly over breakfast. He passed the newspaper to Raf Di Salis, who was staying with them again. 'Her father's Robert West, of course, the South African media tycoon.'

The Count returned some non-committal reply, but Emily was aware that he was watching her across the table. Which made it utterly essential that she stayed in her seat, eating her toast as if it was all that mattered, when what she really wanted was to escape to her room and give way to the tears tightening in her chest.

But she could not—would not break down in front of Raf Di Salis, of all people.

I hate him, she thought childishly. I hate him for being here. For—knowing how I must feel, because he might just pity me, and that would be unbearable.

But when Simon eventually did return, he had no wife with him, tycoon's daughter or not. It was Emily herself who had been married for over two years. And she was hesitant at first when Simon rang and asked if he could see her.

'Nothing heavy, Em,' he persuaded. 'Just a chat about old times over a drink.' He paused. 'Unless your husband would object.'

She said curtly, 'He's not here to express an opinion,' and the die was cast.

Simon had been frank about his engagement, which had been broken after only a few months.

'It was never right with Rebecca,' he said. 'And I always knew it. Her father encouraged me because her previous fiance had a cocaine habit, and I seemed marginally more acceptable.

'Plus it had also been made clear to me that your father had very different plans for you. That, all along, he intended you for his aristocratic Italian financier and I had no chance. By asking Rebecca to marry me, I was trying to prove to myself that I didn't care. That I'd moved on. And when I heard you'd actually married Rafaele Di Salis, I felt almost justified.'

He shook his head. 'But it was hopeless, because I knew in my heart that nothing would ever change the way I felt about you.'

He shot her a keen glance. 'People in the village say that he's hardly ever around. That you rarely see him.'

'No,' she said. 'Apart from the gossip columns and the pictures in glossy magazines.'

He didn't pretend to misunderstand. 'Doesn't that hurt you?'

She shrugged. 'No, why should it? I didn't marry for love and, as soon as I'm twenty one, the trust will end and I can get a divorce.'

He was staring at her as if he'd never seen her before. 'My God, Em.' His voice was barely a whisper as his hand closed round hers. 'Are you saying you're going to be free quite soon—and that you and I might get a second chance?'

She disengaged herself gently. 'I can't possibly say that. It's far too soon and too much has happened.'

He said quietly, 'I want you back, darling. I should have stayed and fought for you, but I had so little to offer. But now I'll move heaven and earth to get you back, so be warned.'

And now he has me back, Emily told herself. And we can consign the last three years to well-deserved oblivion, and—be happy.

Starting now, she thought, as she heard the chime of the front doorbell. She uncoiled herself from the chair, smiling in anticipation as she walked across the room and out into the hall, where Mrs Penistone was admitting the newcomer.

'Simon, how nice.' She offered her cheek for his kiss, aware of the housekeeper's faint disapproval. In the older woman's eyes, Emily was still a married woman even if her marriage had never been conducted on conventional lines. 'Penny, we'll have lunch in half an hour.'

'Yes, madam,' was the dour reply as Mrs Penistone retreated.

Simon followed Emily into the drawing room and closed the door behind them.

'Darling,' he said fervently and took her in his arms, kissing her passionately. As he raised his head at last, he smiled down at her. 'All intruders dealt with?' he asked breathlessly. 'The divorce papers safely signed?'

Emily freed herself gently and moved to one of the sofas. 'Not—exactly.'

'But surely they brought them?' Simon seated himself beside her.

'Probably. I didn't ask.' She hesitated. 'You see, I've decided against a divorce.'

'What?' The word seemed to explode into the air. 'What the hell are you talking about? Are you saying you've changed your mind about marrying me?'

There was a sharpness bordering on anger in his voice that she'd never heard before.

'Of course not.' She stroked his cheek with a placatory hand. 'It's nothing like that. It just occurred to me that it would be much quicker and simpler if I got an annulment. So I opted for that instead.'

Simon drew a deep, unsteady breath. 'And you told them this? You—actually said it to your husband's lawyers?'

'Naturally.' Emily paused. 'I can't say they were best pleased, but I convinced them I was in earnest and they've now gone off to break the news to their lord and master.'

There was a silence, then Simon said hoarsely, 'Have you gone mad? Are you completely off your bloody head? You've sent a message to a man like Raf Di Salis that you want rid of him on the grounds of non-consummation?' His voice rose. 'Tell me this is a joke—please.'

Emily's brows snapped together. 'I couldn't be more serious. It's a far more honest way of ending this travesty than a divorce— especially the no-fault variety Raf is pushing for.' She lifted her chin. 'He should think himself lucky. After all, I could be citing all the women that he *has* slept with since our marriage.'

'Well, you certainly didn't want him, so why the hell should you care how he spends his nights?' Simon got to his feet and began to pace the room restlessly, his face like thunder. 'For God's sake, Em, call the lawyers back. Tell them you've had second thoughts, before it's too late, and that you'll sign anything they want.'

'Why should I?'

He said bluntly, 'Because when Di Salis hears you're asking for an annulment, it will be like a red rag to a bull. And you don't want him angry, Em. Really you don't.'

For a moment Emily remembered Signor Mazzini's warning about throwing down the gauntlet and felt chilled. But she rallied, saying with an assumption of lightness. 'Poor Simon. What on earth did he do three years ago to scare you so?'

He flushed angrily. 'He didn't do anything, in the way you mean. He didn't even say much—because he didn't have to. It's just—the way he is. Maybe you haven't seen the ruthless side of him, Em', he added. 'But it's there, just below the surface. And I wouldn't deliberately upset him any more than I'd poke a sleeping tiger with a stick.'

'But why should he be upset?' Emily shrugged. 'He certainly doesn't want me either, so why the hell should he care how the marriage ends, just as long as it does?'

'Because I don't think it'll be that simple. Not with him.' Simon paused. 'God—you didn't mention me in all this, did you?'

Emily's frown deepened at the anxiety in his voice. 'Not by name, but I made it clear I planned to remarry. I'm not ashamed of that. Or of you, for that matter.' She took a deep breath. 'And I also think it's time that Count Di Salis realised he can't always have his own way.'

She paused. 'And now let's have a drink. I asked Penny to put some champagne on ice to celebrate the morning's achievements, but maybe you'd prefer a large Scotch instead.'

'Make it a treble,' Simon said moodily. 'And have one yourself. Because I'm telling you now, Em, before this business is finished you're going to need it.'

CHAPTER THREE

'I WON'T see him,' Emily said stormily. 'I *will not*.'

'And just how,' Simon asked, 'do you plan to avoid him?'

'I don't know. But I'll find some way.' She looked at the piece of paper crumpled in her hand. 'As soon as I received his letter I wrote back, making it perfectly clear that I wouldn't meet him under any circumstances. That any discussion must be conducted only through our lawyers.'

'Hell's bells.' Simon sounded startled. 'Surely you don't expect old Henshaw to handle this kind of thing? It would be the death of him.'

'Of course not,' Emily returned irritably. 'He's Raf's co-trustee, for heaven's sake. Thinks the sun shines out of him. No, I was planning to hire some big-hitter from London. Someone who won't run scared of the great Count Di Salis.

'And now—today—I get back from shopping,' she added furiously, 'to find this—this bloody telephone message, saying that he's arriving in England in forty-eight hours time and I can expect to see him the following day.'

She swallowed. 'What's worse, he actually dared to tell Penny that he couldn't wait to see me again, and now she's being all arch and asking which room she should prepare for him, and what would he like for dinner?'

'I didn't know she was such a romantic,' Simon muttered.

Emily glared at him. 'He flirts with her,' she said stonily. 'Outrageously.' She shook her head. 'Oh, God, Simon, what am I going to do? And please don't say "I told you so."'

Simon was silent for a moment. 'Have you called him back?'

She shook her head. 'I came straight here to ask your advice.'

Simon chewed on his lip. He seemed, Emily thought, as much on edge as she was herself.

'Why not get in touch with him?' he said at last. 'See if you can head him off by agreeing to his quickie divorce.'

'Never,' she said fiercely.

'But what other solution is there—apart from running away, of course?'

Emily lifted her head and stared at him. 'Simon,' she said. 'Darling, you're a genius.' She nodded, her eyes narrowing. 'When he arrives, I just won't be there. Penny can tell him quite truthfully that I've gone away for an indefinite period and left no forwarding address.'

Her mouth curled. 'The world of finance is bound to collapse without him, so he won't want to hang around, waiting for my return. Apart from anything else, it would make him look very silly,' she added reflectively.

'And, as soon as he's out of the way again, I can get the annulment started.' She gave a small exultant laugh. 'Everything beautifully sorted.'

'But where will you go?' Simon asked. 'You haven't got long to decide.'

'Somewhere that he won't even dream of looking.' She thought for a moment, her bottom lip caught in her teeth. 'I can't use my passport, of course. I'm sure he could trace me. So it will have to be some incredibly unlikely place in this country.'

There was another silence, then Simon said slowly, 'Actually, I might be able to help you there. Some people I know have a weekend cottage in Scotland—a village miles from anywhere called Tullabrae. They rent the place out when they're not using it.'

'Scotland?' Emily repeated. 'I don't suppose Raf even knows where that is.' She looked at him, her eyes sparkling. 'Is it empty at the moment?'

Simon looked towards the window, at the expanse of wintry sky, and pulled a face. 'Almost certainly, I'd say.'

'God, it could save my life.' She thought rapidly. 'I could rent it for two weeks. That will give Raf plenty of time to give me up as a bad job and go back to Paris or Hong Kong or wherever he's operating from at the moment.' She put an eager hand on his arm. 'Could you contact them for me—make the arrangements? Tell them I'll pay cash.'

He looked down at the carpet. 'Yes—I suppose so.' His tone sounded strange. 'If that's what you really want.'

'Well, of course it is.' She was puzzled. 'It sounds ideal. And as you say, I haven't much time.'

He made no reply and she looked at him, frowning a little. 'Darling, is something wrong? You've been odd ever since I got here.'

'I'm sorry.' He summoned a smile. 'It's just—Scotland in January. The weather could be tricky.'

'All the better,' Emily said triumphantly. 'Count Di Salis prefers his snow in the Italian Alps, designer style. The domestic kind won't appeal to him at all.'

For a moment he hesitated, then got to his feet. 'Then I'll email them now. Make the deal.' He paused at the door. 'Shall I ask Tracey to bring you a hot drink? I won't specify the flavour, as everything tastes like dishwater.'

Emily wrinkled her nose. 'Thanks, my love, but no thanks.' She hesitated. 'Have you told your aunt and uncle yet that Mrs Whipple left? I bet they're devastated after all these years. I know how I'd feel if Penny gave notice.'

'I haven't said anything yet. They're having such a great time on their trip, I don't want to spoil things. And I'll hire someone else before they get back.'

Left alone, Emily looked around her. The drawing room at High Gables had always been a gracious room, with its beautiful Chinese carpet and pastel furnishings, but since the housekeeper's departure it was beginning to look shabby and unloved. Bare too, she thought, with faint puzzlement. The Georgian candlesticks were missing from the mantelpiece and the bow-fronted cabinet containing Celia Aubrey's prized collection of Meissen figurines seemed half-empty.

It still seemed incredible that Mrs Whipple should have left while her employers were on their holiday of a lifetime, visiting relatives and old friends on a leisurely trip that would take them all round the world.

And even worse that her place had been taken by Tracey Mason, even temporarily, who'd been sacked as a barmaid from the Red Lion for poor timekeeping and general laziness.

And with no one to keep an eye on her except Simon, who was house-sitting in the Aubreys' absence and running his own import business from High Gables at the same time.

But, although he might jib at Tracey's coffee, manlike, he probably didn't notice unpolished furniture and smeared windows, or tally the amount of breakages.

I hope he does look for a permanent replacement for her soon, Emily thought with a sigh, because the house is beginning to look really sad now.

As though its pulse had stopped beating. And that wouldn't have happened in Mrs Whipple's day.

Much as Emily had grieved for her father, she'd been determined, after his death, to see that the Manor remained just as it had been, with all the gracious charm he'd loved, setting her face resolutely against any suggestions of further modernisation. And, although it galled her to admit it, Raf Di Salis had accepted her stance and allowed her to have her way.

She got up restively and went to the window. I don't want to give him credit, she thought, but in this case I have to. He's fulfilled his part of the bargain. And I—I haven't made waves. Or, not until now.

She sometimes wondered if she hadn't been pressured into becoming his wife—if he'd simply acted as her trustee— whether they could have managed some semblance of a working relationship.

In the months before the bombshell of her father's terminal illness had burst on her, she might not have welcomed Raf's visits but she'd almost become accustomed to them.

And when she'd been summoned home from school in the middle of the summer term to the news that Sir Travers had suddenly collapsed, she'd been almost glad to find him there and had come almost insensibly to rely on his quiet, almost impersonal kindness in the trauma of the weeks that followed.

An inoperable brain tumour, the doctors had told her, their faces compassionate. And only a matter of time…

'I've changed my will,' Sir Travers said one afternoon when she was sitting with him. 'You'll still inherit everything I have to leave, my dearest, but not until you're twenty-one and better able to cope with that kind of responsibility.

'In the meantime, however, I've created a trust and your affairs will be administered by Leonard Henshaw.' He paused. 'And also by Rafaele.'

The breath caught in her throat. 'Oh, no, surely not.' The protest was instinctive. 'Mr Henshaw I can understand, if you think this trust is really necessary, but Count Di Salis is—practically a stranger,' she added stiltedly.

'I thought that lately you'd become friends.'

'Hardly that, although he's been—helpful.'

'Nevertheless, this is my decision and it will stand.' He paused. 'There is one more thing. As my heiress, you could find yourself the target of unscrupulous people and I wish you to be—properly shielded.

'I have discussed this with Rafaele and he has a suggestion to put to you.'

Her heart seemed to stop. 'What—what kind of suggestion?'

'He intends to ask you to become his wife.' He saw the shock in her pale face and put his hand over hers. 'Naturally, he would not expect it to be a marriage in the—conventional sense,' he added awkwardly. 'Because you're still young for that kind of commitment, even if you wished it.' He paused. 'Do you wish it?'

'No,' Emily managed.

Not with him, she thought wildly. Never with him.

'Then, as your husband, Raf would simply become your legal protector for the duration of the trust.' The drawn face smiled a little. 'Keeping the wolves at bay, my darling.'

And who'll keep him at bay? She thought it, but did not say it.

'And when the trust ends?' she questioned tautly.

'Naturally, you would both be free to go your separate ways. I have his word on that.'

Her voice was strained. 'But this can't be what he wants either.'

'Perhaps not,' her father said. 'Let's just say it's his way of repaying an old debt.' He paused. 'Emily, I can't force you to marry Raf Di Salis, but I need to know that when I'm gone, you won't be alone. For my peace of mind, I beg you to accept his proposal. Do this for me, darling—please. I can rest easy only if I know you're being cared for.'

The hoarse words were like nails being driven into her coffin. She said tonelessly, 'If it's—really what you wish...'

'It is.' He patted her hand. 'Go to him, my dear. He's waiting for you in the drawing room.'

Raf was standing by the window when she entered. He looked at her, his face expressionless.

'Your father has told you what I wish to ask?'

'Yes.'

'So—will you be my wife, Emilia?'

'Yes,' she said again.

She thought he was going to come towards her and was suddenly assailed by a vivid memory of his arms holding her, his lips caressing hers. She froze and immediately felt foolish, because he hadn't moved at all. In fact, it was almost as if he'd taken a step backwards, she thought in confusion.

His tone was wintry. 'Then it is settled. You have given your word to me and to your father, which I think is more important.'

She lifted her chin. 'Yes.'

'And he explained the terms of the contract between us? Just nod or shake your head.' His voice bit. 'Spare me another monosyllable.'

Her eyes flashed angrily, but she gave a reluctant nod.

'You clearly expect to be obeyed,' she said coldly. 'I hope you don't require to be loved and honoured too.'

'I am no believer in miracles.' He walked across the room to the door. His faint smile was ironic. 'Now, shall we go to your father and share our good news?'

Remembering, Emily bit her lip. It was the marriage, she thought, that had finally sealed the impenetrable barrier between them.

She had tried to play the minor role in his life assigned to her quietly and dutifully, but it had never been easy—had made her tongue-tied and wary when he was around. And oddly resentful when he wasn't.

And, although he'd adhered strictly to the terms of their arrangement, she'd always been aware of a strange tension between them and felt nervous and on edge whenever she was obliged to be alone with him.

So—I have no intention of ever being alone with him again, she thought, staring at the bare trees outside. And very soon now I won't even have to think about him.

And she wouldn't be looking back at the past now, she told herself, if Raf hadn't forced himself back into her consciousness like this.

She glanced down at her watch, wondering what on earth was keeping Simon all this time. Maybe the cottage wasn't available after all, but there would be others.

And maybe she was wrong to involve him. After all, he'd had one run in with Raf Di Salis already and could well be targeted again, when her husband came looking for her. Perhaps it was the thought of that which was making him so morose—and odd.

She was on her way to the door to say she'd changed her mind when he returned.

'The booking's all made, starting from the day after tomorrow. The caretaker in the village will be informed and have the place ready for you.' He gave her a sheet of paper printed with a detailed description of the cottage and how it could be reached. 'The nearest station is Kilrossan,' he said. 'Let Mrs McEwen know the time of your train and you'll be met.' He paused. 'I made the reservation in your maiden name. I hope that's all right.'

'Entirely appropriate,' she said. 'Under the circumstances.'

She was half-expecting him to offer to go with her. She would refuse, of course. Her marriage vows might be totally meaningless, but, unlike Raf Di Salis, she intended to keep them, even for the short time that was left. And, to give Simon his due, he seemed to accept this, even if he didn't completely understand.

But then, she thought, I'm not sure I understand myself.

She said, 'I'd better go home and start packing. Although I'll have to be careful or Penny will get suspicious.'

'Tell her what she wants to hear,' he said. 'Let her think you're going off to meet your husband, but that it's all to be a huge surprise.'

'Now why didn't I think of that?' She went to him, lifting her face for his kiss. 'Will you be all right—if Raf comes asking questions?'

'He won't,' he said. 'His pride would never stand for it.'

'I'll miss you. Let me know as soon as the coast's clear and I'll come back.'

'And I'll miss you too.' His mouth was suddenly hot and passionate on hers. It was the first real sign of emotion he'd shown that morning and Emily tried to respond with equal ardour. But it wasn't easy when she felt so apprehensive, and eventually she freed herself gently.

'I'm sorry, darling. I can't seem to think of much beyond getting away from here.'

As they walked to the door, his arm round her shoulders, she said, 'By the way, what's happened to the candlesticks?'

'Candlesticks?'

She pointed at the fireplace. 'The lovely silver ones that used to stand right there.'

Simon shrugged indifferently. 'Aunt Celia probably put them away before she left. They'll turn up.'

She looked sideways at him. 'You sound miserable again.'

He looked past her. 'Scotland's a long way and two weeks can seem like for ever.'

'They'll soon pass,' she said. 'Then we'll be together again. And for always this time.'

As her car moved down the drive she turned to wave, but there was no one there and she realised that Simon had gone back in the house, closing the door behind him.

As if, she thought, he could not bear to see her go. Yet, instead of being pleased, she found suddenly that she was shivering. And wondered why.

So far, so good, thought Emily as the express train ate up the miles between London and Glasgow.

Getting away from the Manor had been altogether easier than she'd expected. Penny had swallowed her ludicrous story about meeting Raf in London and beamed at Emily's blush, even though it was inspired by guilt rather than anticipation of a blissful marital reunion.

And yet the housekeeper knew that Emily and Raf had never so much as shared a room when he stayed at the Manor.

Unless she thinks he pays me secret visits when the lights are out, Emily thought, grimacing inwardly.

In fact, the only time Raf had ever entered her bedroom at all had been on their wedding night. And that for the briefest possible time.

Her father had died, quite peacefully, only a week after she'd become engaged. And the wedding had taken place just over a month later, a quiet register office ceremony with Leonard Henshaw and his wife as the only witnesses.

Afterwards, they had flown to Italy for what was supposed to be their honeymoon.

'It is the convention,' Raf said simply when she tried to protest. 'And anyway, I would like to show you my home.' He paused. 'Is that—agreeable to you?'

She swallowed. 'Won't it be very hot in Rome at this time of year?'

'There is a pool,' he said. 'Do you like to swim?'

She had a sudden vision of the pool at High Gables and Simon splashing her, laughing in the sunlight.

She turned away. 'I used to. Not any more.' And thought she heard him sigh.

But she had to admit that the house just outside Rome was beautiful, if a little gloomy, with its marble floors and old-fashioned furniture. It was older even than the Manor and larger too, with a labyrinth of passages and rooms, many of them with ornamental ceilings and frescoed walls, and most of them in need of attention.

It also required a considerable staff to run it and, to Emily's embarrassment, they were all lined up waiting to welcome her in high excitement.

If they only knew, she thought bitterly, that their new Contessa is a total fraud.

And a worried fraud at that, for she seemed to have been assigned the most enormous bedroom, with the largest canopied bed she'd ever seen, and the maids who unpacked for her were exchanging conspiratorial smiles as they arranged her prettiest white nightdress across the embroidered coverlet.

Emily felt her throat tighten in fright. In spite of Raf's assurances, it seemed obvious that the scene was being set for the ritual deflowering of the latest Di Salis bride.

And her nervousness increased when she discovered that, as well as doors to a dressing room and a large bathroom, there was also direct access to an adjoining and equally imposing room, which bore all the signs of male occupation. And realised that, although this door had an ornate lock, there was no key to go with it.

Dinner was served much later than she was accustomed to and, while the food was delicious, she had little appetite for it and none at all for the wine which accompanied it.

She needed, she thought, to stay very, very sober.

And, even if she wasn't hungry, to make the meal last as long as possible.

'You look tired,' Raf commented, as the cheese course was being cleared.

'A little,' she returned cautiously. She was actually dead on her feet but she wasn't going to admit as much.

'It has been a long day,' he said, confirming all her worst fears by adding, 'I suggest you go to bed.' He paused. 'Can you find your way back to your room?'

'Of course,' she said too quickly, in case he offered to escort her.

'If you get lost, call out and eager rescuers will immediately appear.' He smiled at her. 'You are an object of fascination for the entire household, you understand.'

'Yes,' she returned tautly. 'I—gathered that.'

Raf was leaning back in his chair, his lean fingers playing with the stem of his wineglass.

'You looked very lovely today, *mia cara*,' he said quietly. 'Your dress was charming.'

'It—it wasn't new. I wore it when Daddy took me to Ascot one time.' She remembered with a pang how joyously she'd chosen the slender cream silk shift just skimming her knees.

She added stiffly, 'I hope you don't mind.'

'If you had worn it a hundred times, you would have looked no less beautiful.'

The conversation was taking altogether too personal a turn, she decided, and pushed back her chair, pretending to yawn.

'I think maybe you're right and I should call it a day.'

He rose too. 'Then I wish you goodnight.'

She murmured something in reply and went, trying not to hurry too obviously. At least he hadn't attempted to kiss her, she thought, as she went up the wide sweep of staircase. Nor was he following her.

But she breathed more easily when she reached her room and, having stumblingly dismissed the maid who was waiting to assist her, showered and cleaned her teeth in the palatial bathroom, then put on the nightdress that Penny must have substituted for the satin pyjamas she'd intended to bring and climbed up into that monster of a bed.

It was a very comfortable monster, she discovered, and the linen was scented with rose-water. But she couldn't relax. She kept watching the communicating door, asking herself what she would do if it opened, and dreading the moment when she might be called on to make a decision.

But, just when she'd resolved it was safe enough to put out the lamp and get some sleep, she heard a faint noise and looked up to see Raf standing there in the open doorway. He was barefoot, his jacket and tie discarded and his shirt half-unbuttoned, revealing the strong column of his throat and the dark smooth skin of his chest.

For what seemed an eternity they stared at each other. Emily sat transfixed, her heart thudding erratically, her mouth suddenly dry, aware that one lacy strap had slipped down from her shoulder, but not daring to adjust it. Just waiting for him to say something—do something.

But when he moved, it was simply to put out a hand and steady himself against the doorframe. For a terrible moment she thought he was drunk and tensed involuntarily. However, when he spoke his voice was crisp and clear, without slurring.

'Emilia, my household has—expectations about tonight and its usual significance, which may have caused you concern.

'I wish to say that you have no need to fear that I will break my word to you. Today's ceremony changed nothing and our marriage is still a business arrangement which can—will remain in name only, as you wish. Then, when you are twenty one, you will be free to live your own life and—find happiness.'

He made her a slight bow, then he was gone, closing the door firmly behind him.

For a long time, Emily recalled, she'd sat quite still, gazing unseeingly into space, aware only of the still-flurried race of her heart. And when, eventually, she'd reached for the lamp switch, she'd discovered that her hand was shaking uncontrollably.

Just as it was trembling again now, at this moment, as she picked up the carton of coffee in front of her and drank.

Why am I doing this to myself? she asked with a kind of desperation. Remembering all this—stuff. It must be the most pointless exercise of my entire life. Because it changes nothing. It can't...

But perhaps it was something she needed to do, if only to convince herself that the stance she was taking was completely justified. That her relationship with Raf Di Salis had been null and void from the beginning and that it was hypocritical to pretend otherwise.

Although she could quite see that it would be a blow to Raf's *amour-propre* to be forced to admit openly that his wife was not among his numerous conquests.

In fact, he'd been prepared to go to considerable lengths to present a very different picture of their relationship, she recalled, wincing.

It had been the morning after the wedding and it seemed to Emily that she'd only just managed to drop into a restless sleep when she had been woken by a hand on her shoulder and opened heavy eyes to see Raf standing beside the bed.

She'd sat up, pushing back her hair, instantly defensive.

'What do you want?' Her voice was husky.

His mouth tightened. 'To give you this.' He held out a small leather box. 'Open it,' he directed.

She obeyed and gasped when she saw the beautiful square sapphire enclosed by small diamonds that it contained.

'An engagement ring?' She frowned in bewilderment. 'Isn't it a little late for that?'

'It is a family tradition,' he said quietly. 'This ring is given by each Count to his bride on the first day of their honeymoon as a sign that she has pleased him. I wish you to wear it.'

Her face flamed. 'No way.'

'Then I must insist. It will make your situation here much easier if it is thought that we make each other happy. Or that you make me happy.' He looked at her mutinous expression and sighed. 'Emilia, I have spared you the intimacies of marriage to me. Its formalities, however, you will endure, and this is one of them. Do I make myself clear? Now put it on.'

She acceded reluctantly, hoping that it would not fit. But the sapphire slid easily over her knuckle as if it had been made for her alone.

'Are there any other degrading medieval customs I should know about?' she asked haughtily.

'If I think of any, I will tell you.' He paused. 'Now go back to sleep.' He added wryly, 'You will not be disturbed again.' And left her.

To her own astonishment, she fell asleep within minutes and it was nearly midday when she awoke next time.

She bathed and dressed hastily, conscious all the time of the unfamiliar weight of the sapphire on her hand and its distasteful significance. And it took nearly all the courage she possessed to present herself downstairs, knowing she would be under scrutiny, however discreet.

Raf's butler, a stately individual called Gaspare, was waiting for her in the hall to conduct her out on to the terrace at the rear of the house where Raf was seated at a table under an awning.

'*Carissima*.' His voice was warm and filled with laughter as he got to his feet and came to her. Under Gaspare's indulgent gaze, he took the hand that wore his ring and kissed it, then bent, brushing her cheek with his lips.

It was the lightest of touches, but she flinched just the same and saw his eyes harden.

'Another formality,' he said softly, as he straightened. 'Accustom yourself.'

And she'd nodded, unable to speak.

And formal was how their relationship had remained in every respect, for which she could only be grateful. True to his word, Raf had never visited her bedroom again, or attempted to make physical demands on her in any way.

But that had been an easy promise to a girl who was too

young and inexperienced to appeal to his sophisticated tastes anyway, she reminded herself tautly. Someone he'd been saddled with, simply because he owed her dying father.

It occurred to her that, for a supposed honeymoon, there had been very little privacy, although Raf himself seemed unaware or uncaring of the fact that they were the cynosure of all eyes.

Not that they were together that much, and she was thankful that the house and its gardens were vast enough for her to be able to make herself scarce most of the time. After all, she had the excuse that she was exploring her new surroundings.

But there were times when she was obliged to be in his company and she found this a strain, conscious always of his cool politeness. At mealtimes in particular, because there were servants present, she struggled, trying to respond to his efforts to engage her in conversation and to smile back at him as if she was really the fulfilled and loving bride of everyone's expectations.

Perhaps the most successful times were the days when he took her into Rome with him, showing her all the usual tourist sights, but also allowing her a glimpse of his own city, the hidden side that the visiting swarms never saw.

But she was relieved when the supposed honeymoon ended and she was able to fly back to Britain. Although even this had its awkward moment.

Raf had ordered champagne on the flight and, when it came, he raised his glass in a toast to her.

'I am proud of you, *mia cara*,' he told her quietly. 'It cannot have been easy for you.'

'Thank you.' Emily did not look at him. 'It wasn't—that bad—in the end. And your house is wonderful,' she added stiltedly. 'But I'll be glad to be home again and get back to normal life.'

He was silent for a moment. 'Do I take it you will be in no hurry to return to Italy?' His tone was mildly curious.

'Well, that wasn't part of the deal, was it?' she returned defensively. 'I thought I'd be living in England.'

'Of course, if that is what you wish.' He paused again. 'Perhaps I was hoping, Emilia, that even if we are not lovers, we might become—friends. Learn to enjoy being together. What do you think?'

'That it's not very likely. After all, we come from totally different worlds, and you have a very busy life.' She stared at the bubbles rising in her glass as if they fascinated her. 'You don't have to be kind. Really. I'll be fine.'

'But there will be times when we shall be obliged to meet,' he said curtly. 'When I shall need you to act as my hostess. I did explain this to you.'

'Yes,' she said. 'The formalities again.' She paused. 'But you don't have to worry. I'll do my best to carry out my duties to your satisfaction.'

'*Grazie, mia sposa.*' His voice was ironic, almost harsh. 'Then that is how it shall be.'

And that was how it had been, Emily told herself. At first, Raf's visits to England had been frequent and his calls on her services quite exacting, but as the months had passed they'd become more and more rare.

And at the same time, she'd discovered the first newspaper stories of his liaison with one of the Italian film industry's rising young stars, Luisa Danni.

For a while she'd felt stunned. But, after all, what else could she reasonably have expected? Just because she preferred to sleep alone, there was no reason for Raf to be celibate too, she told herself over and over again. That had never been part of the deal.

So there would be no accusations—no recriminations. No reproaches either. In fact, no reaction at all.

She would continue to be polite and pleasant when she saw him, play the part required of her when necessary, and try not to think about him at all when he was absent.

Besides, if she said anything, it might seem as if she cared. As if his infidelity actually mattered to her. And that wasn't true. It wasn't true at all.

So she would ignore the whole sordid situation and simply live for the time when she would no longer be his unwanted wife. When she would be free of him.

And that time, thought Emily, staring through the train window at the flying countryside, that time is now.

My marriage is over and there's nothing on this earth that Raf Di Salis can do about it.

CHAPTER FOUR

IT WAS dark when Emily got to Glasgow, and pitch black when she arrived at last at Kilrossan. But her journey, though lengthy, had run like clockwork and she'd had no trouble making her connection.

As she descended on to the cold and windy platform and stood for a moment ruefully easing her spine, a rangy young man approached out of the gloom.

'You'll be Miss Blake, I'm thinking.' Voice and smile were cheerful. 'I have the Jeep waiting.'

He took the suitcase crammed with warm clothing and the bag of books from her and set off towards the exit.

'I'm Angus McEwen, by the way,' he added. 'It's my auntie who looks after the cottage for the owners, although there aren't many visitors at this time of year.'

'I wanted to find somewhere quiet and remote,' Emily told him, huddling gratefully into her fleece.

He laughed. 'Well, it's that all right.'

'It's also absolutely freezing!'

'There's snow expected.' He stowed her bags in the back of the Jeep and they set off.

She said stiltedly, 'It's very good of you to come and collect me at this time in the evening.'

'All part of the service. I'm home on leave and like to keep occupied.' He paused. 'How did you hear about the cottage?'

'Through a friend.'

'It's a shame it's so dark because the scenery around here's something grand,' he told her. 'Mind you, they say the desert's beautiful too, but I can't see it myself.'

'Is that where you work?'

He nodded. 'I started on the oil rigs but now I'm on a contract in Saudi.' He paused again. 'Are you a walker, Miss Blake? Because, if you're planning to head into the hills at some point, you'll need to leave a message with Auntie at the shop about where you're going and when you reckon to be back. Snow or not, the weather can still be treacherous at this time of year and getting the mountain rescue team out is expensive.'

Emily smiled. 'Don't worry,' she said. 'I've come to relax.' *Or try to...* 'I'm not tackling more than the odd gentle stroll.'

'Then I'd better give you a bit of peace now,' Angus commented ruefully. 'The family always say I could talk the hind leg off of a donkey.'

If she was truthful, Emily was glad of the silence. She still couldn't believe her escape had been so simple. The only query had come from the ticket office clerk at the station. 'A first class single to London, madam? Not a return?'

She'd smiled demurely. 'I'll probably be coming back by car,' she fibbed. She wouldn't, of course, but if Raf made enquiries that was what he'd be told. And from London she could have gone anywhere.

She didn't even want to contemplate what his reaction would be when he arrived at the Manor and discovered she was missing. But she wouldn't worry about that now. She had two weeks of solitary bliss in which to make her contingency plans. And when she returned she'd be ready for anything.

They seemed to have been driving for ever but at last the Jeep turned off and Emily found they were bumping over a rutted uphill track.

Her companion pointed to a light ahead of them. 'That's Braeside Cottage. Auntie'll have been up with a welcome pack— bread, milk, porridge oats and the like. And I'm to show you where everything is and light the living room fire for you.

'The water and heating work off oil,' he went on as Emily murmured appreciatively. 'And the cooker uses bottled gas, because the electricity goes off sometimes in bad weather. But

Auntie Maggie makes sure there's always a good stock of candles.' He paused doubtfully. 'You're certain you won't mind being up here on your own?'

'Believe me,' Emily said truthfully, 'I can hardly wait.'

The cottage was certainly worth waiting for, she thought, as she was ushered straight in through a front door which, Angus told her, was rarely, if ever, locked.

Well, it was the back of beyond, just as she'd hoped, she reminded herself. Her Scottish sanctuary, hundreds of miles from irate Italian millionaires.

It was a large room, comfortably furnished but not flash. Two big sofas upholstered in blue flowered chintz flanked the fireplace and there was a small dining table and two chairs under the window. None of the furniture was new, but it gleamed and there was a pleasing scent of polish in the air.

A curtained archway led to a small but well-equipped kitchen at the rear, with the promised welcome pack standing on one of the counter tops.

In addition, there was a flight of wooden stairs to the upper floor and a door in the corner which Angus said led down to the cellar, where the boiler and the coal bunker were both located.

He took her case upstairs and deposited it in the large front bedroom. Emily saw that there was a thick quilt in a green and white striped cover on the double bed and that the lace-edged pillows were crisply laundered. It looked so inviting that she almost ached.

There were sheepskin rugs on the wooden floor and plain curtains in the same green at the windows. There was also an elderly chest of drawers with a mirror above it and a walk-in cupboard with a hanging rail.

Opposite was a single room, chastely furnished in white, and at the end of the narrow landing was a small but serviceable bathroom with a deep old-fashioned tub and a hand shower.

It was all immaculately clean and shining, which made Angus's Aunt Maggie a treasure. Pity she can't sort out High Gables for Simon, she thought, and wondered if he was missing her, at the same time disturbingly aware that she'd hardly spared him a thought. That she'd been preoccupied with Raf instead, and to an absurd degree. Well, that would stop right now.

When she rejoined Angus downstairs, the fire was already crackling in the grate.

'The kindling's kept in the cellar, too, for dryness,' he mentioned. 'And the log store's in a lean-to at the side of the house. There was a load delivered before Christmas, so don't stint yourself. And it draws well, this fire, so it's easy to light.

'You'll have no trouble finding the village, either,' he continued. 'Just keep walking downhill. Auntie's shop is only open for papers tomorrow, because of the Sabbath. But, if you look in the fridge, you'll find she's left you a Sunday dinner, so you won't starve. I'm afraid that's extra,' he added a touch awkwardly. 'Is that all right?'

'I'm truly grateful,' Emily assured him. 'Your aunt's gone to a lot of trouble to make me welcome, and so have you.'

'Och, think nothing of it.' Angus stood up, dusting his hands. 'Make sure you use the spark guard before you go to bed and you'll be fine.'

'I'm sure I will. I'll just have a quick supper, then sleep off the journey.'

His smile warmed her again. 'Then I'll see you around.'

And he was gone, and she heard the Jeep disappearing down the track.

At last, there was nothing but silence. Emily stood for a moment, looking round her new domain with profound satisfaction.

It was settling in time. She would unpack, make her first meal, take her first bath, then let the stresses and strains of the past week slide away in that big, comfortable bed upstairs.

It felt chilly in the bedroom. She felt the radiator, but it was cold, as was the one in the bathroom. Presumably the heating worked on a timer and had switched itself off, she thought, putting away her clothes in double-quick time.

In the kitchen, she unloaded the groceries in the welcome pack. As Angus had indicated, there was a fresh chicken in the fridge, along with some carrots and a small cabbage.

But, for now, she would make do with a can of soup, and tomato at that, she thought, operating the ring-pull on the can. The ultimate comfort food.

When it was hot, she poured it into a large pottery mug and carried it into the living room. As she sat down one of the logs in the grate collapsed, making her jump, emphasising her awareness of the cottage's isolation.

It seemed strange to have no real idea of the landscape outside the dark rectangle of window, she thought with sudden unease. Maybe it would help if she drew the thick woven cream curtains, closing out the darkness and the unknown together.

But this is what you wanted—a hiding place with total seclusion, she argued inwardly. So why be a wuss about it?

As she began tugging the heavy folds into place, she became aware of two things. That snowflakes were dancing in the air, just as Angus had predicted. And that she could hear the sound of an engine and see a pair of powerful headlights approaching the cottage.

Oh, God, she thought, groaning inwardly. Surely it wasn't Angus paying another visit on some pretext. He didn't seem the type to make a nuisance of himself because she was female and on her own, but how did she know? What did she know?

She would just have to make it perfectly plain that she didn't need any kind of complication in her life. And, whatever he'd said earlier, she'd keep that damned door locked.

But, even as she turned to do so, she heard a vehicle door slam and footsteps approaching on the gravelled area just outside.

As the cottage door opened, she said breathlessly, 'Whatever you have to say can wait until tomorrow. Now, I'd just like you to go.'

'But how inhospitable of you, *carissima*,' came the drawled reply. 'Particularly when I have come so far to find you.'

And, as Emily halted in stunned disbelief, Raf Di Salis stepped into the lamplit room.

Emily couldn't speak. She could hardly think. She just stood there, rooted to the spot, staring at him. Watching him strip off his gloves.

He can't be here, she thought. It wasn't possible for him to have found out her destination and followed her so quickly. Yet he was only too real.

There were snowflakes clinging to his dark hair and to the shoulders of the parka he was wearing and he was carrying a leather travel bag, which he allowed to drop to the floor with a thud that sounded ominously final.

'Lost for words, *mia bella*?' he asked, the hazel eyes raking her mercilessly. 'How strange. You seemed eloquent enough when you spoke to my lawyers the other day. And very frank.'

Her throat closed in fright as she remembered every reckless word she'd thrown at them. His arrival had made the cottage seem suddenly smaller and more cramped. And there was a note of cold, quiet anger in his voice that made her shiver.

He noticed instantly. 'You are cold, my angel? Forgive me.' He kicked the door shut behind him. 'So, Emilia, are you pleased with the cottage?'

She found her voice at last. 'I was—until a moment ago.' She took a deep breath. 'What the *hell* are you doing here?'

'I have come to talk to you, *naturalmente*,' Raf said softly. 'To discuss your recent ultimatum—among other things. I told you so in my letter. And you must have received it, or why would you be here?'

'I came because I chose not to see you—not to have this conversation.' She tried to keep her voice steady as her mind ran in crazy circles, trying desperately not to think what she was thinking. 'As you must have known.'

He shrugged. 'But that was not your choice to make.' He unzipped his parka and tossed it across the back of a sofa. Underneath he was wearing a black roll-necked sweater and his long legs were encased in blue denim and tough-looking boots.

He too, it seemed, had dressed for bad weather—and a long stay. And a voice in her head was silently screaming, *No*...

'I made my wishes clear to you, Emilia,' he went on. 'You should have listened.'

'Ah,' she said. 'We're back to the old obedience issue.'

'There are a number of issues,' he said. 'In time, we shall deal with them all.'

'No,' she said angrily. 'I came here to get away from you, as you're clearly aware. Either you leave or I do.'

He walked to the door and opened it again. A flurry of snow

blew in on a wind that seemed to come straight from the Arctic Circle. 'Then go, *mia cara*. I hope you have a destination in mind, because it is not a night to be homeless.'

He paused. 'Or you could be sensible and accept that this interview is inevitable. Which is it to be?'

There was a silence, then Emily turned away almost blindly, wrapping her arms round her body.

'You are wise,' he said and closed the door.

She said, 'How did you know where I'd be?'

'I think you already know the answer to that.'

She said fiercely, 'I suppose you must have forced it out of poor Simon somehow.'

'No force was needed,' he said. 'I have known about this house for a long time. My friends originally offered it to me for our honeymoon and I regret now that I did not accept.' He looked round him appraisingly. 'It is charming and ideally secluded, don't you think?'

The sensation that she was standing on the edge of a precipice was so vivid that Emily almost swayed. She made her way to the sofa and sat down.

'Friends?' she echoed hoarsely. 'What friends?'

'Marcello and Fiona Albero,' he said casually. 'You met them in London when he was at the Embassy, but I knew you would not remember. You were always too enclosed in your little private block of ice, *mia sposa*, to care about any of the people I introduced to you.'

That, she thought indignantly, is *so* unfair, but she could not deal with it now.

She swallowed. 'Then Simon must know them too.'

'Signor Aubrey,' he said with distaste, 'knew only what I told him to say and what I told him to do. You see, I guessed, Emilia *mia*, that you would wish to avoid me if you could. Acting under my instructions, he provided you with the means to do so.'

He paused. 'And he sent you here. To me.'

'No,' she said. 'He wouldn't do that. We—we'd found each other again, Simon and I. We had plans…' Her voice tailed away, then she rallied. 'You must have tricked him.'

'Of course.' There was harsh mockery in his tone. 'I tricked him into allowing me to pay the worst of his debts. They were considerable.'

'How did you know he owed money?'

'I promised your father I would protect you,' Raf said. 'Therefore, I needed to know what Signor Aubrey was doing—especially when he ignored an earlier warning and came back into your life—with his plans.'

She gasped. 'You mean you've been having him—watched? Investigated?'

'Of course.' His tone was brisk. 'I have to be away a great deal, so how else could I obtain the information I needed? And the money he owed featured prominently in the reports I received.'

'That's nonsense,' Emily said, her voice shaking. 'Simon has his own successful business.'

'There is no business. He has only what his wits can provide,' Raf said curtly. 'And he is running out of options.' He shrugged. 'I did not choose that you should be one of them.'

'Do you know what you're saying?' she whispered. 'You're telling me that the man I love only wanted me because I'm my father's heiress.'

'Yes, Emilia, I am telling you exactly that.'

'And what about me?' she asked, dry-mouthed. 'Have I been—watched too—in your absence?'

'*Si, naturalmente.*'

'I don't think there's anything natural about it,' she said furiously. 'How dared you spy on me?'

'I am a rich man, Emilia, and you are my wife. In some circles this would make you a target.' He shrugged. 'I knew you would not accept a bodyguard at the Manor, so I chose the only alternative.'

'And all from the most altruistic motives, of course.' She radiated scorn. 'But who watches you, pray?'

'I can look after myself,' he said. 'You, I wished to keep safe in accordance with my promise to your father.' He paused. 'Also, I needed to prevent you from making a fool of yourself over Simon Aubrey.'

There was a taut silence, then he added curtly, 'I regret that I have had to distress you. But it is time you knew the whole truth.'

'I don't—I won't believe you.' She snatched up her shoulder bag, extracting her mobile phone. 'I'm going to call Simon right now. Prove you a liar.'

'Then do so,' Raf said and picked up his bag. 'But first tell me where I will be sleeping.'

'You're not staying here.' She looked up, white-faced, her eyes blazing. 'Do you think I'd have you under the same roof?'

His voice was level. 'It is not the first time. And I fail to see how you can stop me.' He paused. 'Fiona told me there are two bedrooms. Do I turn left or right at the top of the stairs?'

Their glances met—clashed, and it was Emily who looked away first, realising he was totally determined.

'To the right,' she said icily. 'I suppose. As, sadly, I'm not physically capable of throwing you out. But Simon can, and he will, when he finds out what you've been saying. He'll be here tomorrow.'

'Your faith is admirable,' he said quietly, 'but misplaced. However, make your call if you must. But first ask yourself this. If I am a liar, how is it that I have found you so easily?'

Emily watched him walk up the stairs, her mind whirling in circles.

She could hardly comprehend what he'd said. It was too monstrous to be true. She couldn't give it credence.

Simon loves me, she thought, and Raf's got a grudge against him because of those stupid things I said to the lawyers about getting married again. That's all it is. It has to be.

And yet she couldn't escape the memory of Simon's odd behaviour the other day—the edgy, reluctant way he'd offered his assistance. As if he felt guilty—or ashamed…

When Raf returned ten minutes later she was still sitting in the same place, the phone dangling from her fingers.

'Well?' he enquired curtly.

She shook her head. 'I can't get through. There's no network available. It must be the mountains.' She looked around. 'There has to be another phone somewhere.'

'Only in the village.' He shrugged. 'Marcello and Fiona prefer to be here alone—without interruptions.'

The word 'alone' seemed to sound in her mind like a knell. It suddenly occurred to her that whenever she and Raf had been together in the past there'd been other people around. Quite apart from acquaintances and guests, everywhere she'd stayed with him had resident staff of some kind.

Now, for the first time, it was—just the two of them, occupying a relatively small space. 'Without interruptions' he'd said. And the realisation sent chills through her.

Raf was prowling the room, inspecting everything, glancing at the books and ornaments on the shelves that flanked the fireplace. He picked up the mug of cold soup and regarded it with disfavour. 'Is this supposed to be supper?'

'Mine, yes,' she said. 'I'm not very hungry.'

'But I am. So—what else is there to eat?'

Emily gasped. 'You really think I'm going to get you a meal?'

He said softly, 'You're still my wife, *mia cara*, and, until now, your duties have not been too onerous. Besides, most wives cook for their husbands—or hadn't you heard?' He paused. 'But maybe you are devoid of culinary skills.'

She said indignantly, 'Everyone at my school learned to cook. The nuns insisted.'

'Ah, the nuns,' Raf said reflectively. 'That explains a great deal. But at least some aspects of your education have received attention, if not all.'

Emily lifted her chin. 'And what is that supposed to mean?'

'It is not important. Are there eggs? You could prepare a simple omelette, perhaps?'

'I could,' she said. 'But why should I?'

'Because a man needs to conduct negotiations on a full stomach,' Raf said smoothly. 'And we are here to negotiate, are we not?'

She took the untouched soup from him with a mutinous look, then stalked with it into the kitchen, pouring it away down the sink. Under the circumstances, she thought, the word 'comfort', even applied to food, was a sick joke.

She filled the kettle and set it to boil. Tea bags and a small jar of instant coffee had been included in the welcome pack, although she couldn't imagine Raf relishing either. But then, he wasn't a welcome guest, so why should she care?

She found a shallow frying pan, added a knob of butter and

placed it on the stove to heat gently. She was breaking eggs into a bowl when Raf came in.

She didn't look at him. 'Do you mind? This is a very small kitchen.'

'I came to bring you this.' He put a package on the worktop beside her.

With chagrin, Emily recognised an expensive brand of freshly ground coffee. She said coolly, 'You think of everything, *signore*.'

'I need to, *carissima*, when I have you to deal with.' He reached a long arm up to a top shelf and took down a box she hadn't even noticed, extracting a cafetière. 'There is no espresso machine, unfortunately, but this will do.'

He rinsed it out and began to spoon in the coffee.

'Do you want two eggs or three?' Emily asked, adding seasoning.

'Four,' he said. 'I need to keep my strength up, don't you agree, my lovely wife?'

Caught unawares, she turned her head sharply, staring at him. 'What do you mean?'

His mouth twisted mockingly. 'Merely, that if it continues to snow like this, I might have to dig us out—what else?' He added laconically, 'And your butter is about to burn,' and went back into the living room.

Gritting her teeth, she moved the pan off the heat and slotted wholemeal bread into the toaster. She filled the cafetière and took china and cutlery through to the living room.

Raf was lounging on a sofa, staring into the newly replenished fire.

She said curtly, 'You do realise there's no television here? No computer or fax machine either. '

'You feel that is a problem?'

She shrugged. 'It's hardly the streamlined, high-tech, luxurious environment you're used to. You can hardly test the world's financial pulse from here.'

'Oh, I think the patient will live without me.'

'But can you live without the patient?'

'For a while, certainly.' He stretched indolently. 'And it will be good for me to relax completely. It does not often happen.'

'You've forgotten the negotiations.'

'I have forgotten nothing,' he said and resumed his scrutiny of the leaping flames, leaving her to retire, baffled.

Emily beat the eggs with a fork and poured them into the hot pan, watching them with an eagle eye to ensure they did not become leathery. But they looked pretty good, fluffy and golden, she decided with satisfaction, as she divided them up, giving Raf the lion's share.

'This is excellent,' he commented after his first mouthful. 'You have hidden talents, *mia cara.*'

She kept her eyes fixed on her plate. 'Let's hear it for Sister Mary Antony.'

She had to force down her own portion against the nervous tightness of her throat, but somehow she managed it. Because it was important not to show she was on edge in front of Raf. Shock and anger at his unexpected arrival were permissible— just—but being scared was not.

Cool indifference, she thought, was the thing to aim for.

The meal over, she refused politely his equally courteous offer to assist with the washing-up. The idea of Rafaele Di Salis with a tea towel in his hand was too ludicrous to contemplate, she decided, her lip curling. More importantly, the kitchen was indeed far too cramped for easy sharing. Especially with him.

When she went back into the living room, she saw, with surprise, that a bottle of wine and two glasses had appeared on the small table in front of him.

'Did you bring that too?' she asked.

'I did not have to. Marcello keeps a small store in the cellar for his own visits.' He poured the wine and handed her a glass. 'He gave me the key to the cupboard.'

'The kind of friend to have,' Emily said with constraint.

She didn't want to sit drinking with him, yet to refuse might send out the wrong sort of signal. So she took a cautious sip and put the glass down.

My God, she thought bitterly, this—ambush had been carefully planned. But it was becoming plain that it couldn't have succeeded without Simon's active connivance, and that this was only one of the ugly truths she might have to accept.

In spite of herself, she couldn't forget the missing items in the drawing room at High Gables and Simon's casual dismissal of her query.

If he was short of money, why didn't he turn to me? she asked herself almost despairingly. Why pretend he was a high-flying entrepreneur working from home, when she was bound to find out the truth eventually?

'You look angry, *carissima*. Is the wine not to your liking?'

'It's fine,' she said. 'However, it doesn't make your invasion of my privacy here any more acceptable.'

He shrugged. 'But then you have never made me particularly welcome, Emilia, wherever you happened to be.'

'Well,' she said, 'that hardly matters. I'm sure you're greeted with open arms everywhere else.'

And could have bitten her tongue out. Because she'd just broken her own cardinal rule and made a reference, however veiled, to the other women in his life.

But Raf did not pick up on it immediately, as she'd feared. He leaned back against the cushions, drinking his wine, his glance meditative. 'It did not occur to you, *mia cara*, that deliberately running away from me might seem—a form of enticement? That I would be bound to follow?'

She stiffened. 'No.'

'How little you know of men,' he murmured.

She tossed back her hair with a fierce gesture. No point in hedging any more and to hell with the consequences. 'I certainly know about you, *signore*,' she said bitingly. 'And I'd have thought you had enough—enticements in your life already.'

She took a deep breath. 'So why don't you say whatever it is you came here for, then get back to your real world? And leave me in peace.'

He looked at her for a long moment, then he got to his feet, picking up his glass and the bottle. 'I suggest we resume this conversation tomorrow,' he said. 'When perhaps you may be more— amenable. More prepared to listen to reason.' He paused. 'Now, am I permitted to take a bath, perhaps, before I retire?'

'Yes, of course.' It was only a small respite, but, as things were, she was thankful for anything. 'You—you'll find extra towels in the airing cupboard, I think.'

'*Grazie*.' He inclined his head courteously. 'I understand that the hot water supply is limited, so I will try not to use it all.'

'I'm sure it's fine,' she returned quickly. 'And your friends obviously manage.'

'Ah,' he said, casually. 'But then they bathe together.' He sent her a swift, impersonal smile, then went unhurriedly up the stairs and out of her sight.

That, thought Emily, furiously aware that she was blushing, was altogether too much information.

Once again, Raf seemed to have caught her on the back foot. And with very little effort on his part.

Why did I think I could ever take him on? she asked herself despondently. I should have hired myself a legal team of my own and let them battle it out.

Only it was too late for that now. He was here, by his own admission, to make her see reason. In other words, to meekly submit to his particular point of view, she thought, biting her lip.

Well, she was damned if she would. She'd fight him every step of the way.

And if he'd imagined that breaking the news of Simon's callous betrayal of her would undermine her strength of will, then he could think again.

When Simon had walked out on her three years ago she'd been devastated, convinced her life was over. Wasn't that why she'd yielded to her father's urgings and agreed to a marriage of convenience with Raf—because she hadn't really cared what happened to her? Wasn't it?

Now it seemed that Simon had really gone for ever. But, instead of the devastation of pain she might have expected, she felt numb—hollowed out inside.

I should be weeping, she thought, her mouth twisting in self-mockery. Maybe I'm just too young for a broken heart.

And, after this, I won't be looking for another man either. Once I'm free of this marriage, I'm going to starting living for myself.

She picked up her neglected wine. 'To me,' she said and drank deeply.

But the fact remained that she was still sharing her living space with Raf, for tonight at least. And, in spite of herself, she found she was sitting on the edge of the sofa, senses finely tuned to the signs of his presence upstairs. That she was tensing as she heard the bath water eventually running away. Listening for the opening of the bathroom door and the soft pad of bare feet going along the passage. Then, at long last, his bedroom door closing.

And that was the most welcome sound of all, she thought, her slim body sagging in relief.

She put the guard in front of the fire and extinguished the lights before going quietly upstairs herself.

She'd expected to find the bathroom a wet-floored shambles, but it was amazingly neat, his damp towel hanging on the hot rail.

There was a small ramshackle bolt on the door, which was more than could be said for her bedroom, and she slid it into place before beginning to refill the tub. Just a precaution, she told herself, and she was probably just being paranoid.

Raf was here on a face-saving exercise, that was all. His male pride had been damaged and perhaps, in retrospect, she'd been unwise to deride it. Maybe it would do no harm to apologise. Explain she'd spoken in the heat of the moment. Show that she could be reasonable.

All the same, her bath was not the long leisurely affair she'd originally planned. She dried herself quickly and put on one of the nightgowns she'd brought with her—a relic from her school-days, voluminous in brushed cotton, but warm, which was all that mattered.

As she went on tiptoe back to her room, she hesitated for a brief moment at the door opposite, but there wasn't a sound. So maybe he was already sound asleep.

She closed her own door and leaned against it, suddenly aware that she'd been holding her breath, listening to the unbroken quiet.

After a moment she went over to the window and drew the curtain aside, wrinkling her nose at the swirl of white flakes dancing in front of her. It seemed to be snowing harder than ever, she thought, and while a sanctuary, however fragile it had proved, was one thing, being stranded by snowdrifts was something else completely.

Shivering, she dashed back to the bed and hopped in, pulling the duvet up to her chin as she waited for the first chill to subside. She stared up at the ceiling, letting thoughts, impressions, snatches of conversation tumble headlong through her mind.

Which achieved precisely nothing, apart from making her feel more on edge than ever. What she really needed was to turn off the lamp and go to sleep, she told herself firmly. Because things always looked better in the morning—didn't they?

And at that moment her door opened with a faint creak and Raf came in. He was wearing a black silk robe, casually belted at the waist, and the rest of him was tawny skin as he moved towards her with an unhurried purpose that brought all her worst fears choking to the surface.

Propped on an elbow, Emily stared at him. 'What—what do you want?'

'We have matters to discuss,' he said. 'If you remember.'

'But tomorrow.' In spite of herself there was a quiver in her voice. 'You said we'd talk tomorrow.'

'It is already tomorrow,' he said. 'And have you never heard of pillow talk?'

His hands went to the sash of his robe and she shrank.

'No,' she said hoarsely. 'No, Raf, please. You can't do this. You promised me…'

'At that time, I was dealing with a terrified child,' he said softly. 'But you told my lawyers that you were planning to remarry, so it seems you have outgrown your virginal fears and are a woman at last.'

'But there'll be no other marriage,' she protested. 'You—you know that.'

His brows lifted. 'And you think that makes a difference? It does not.'

His voice hardened. 'I have been astonishingly patient with you, Emilia, but you went too far with your demand for an annulment. And I intend to make quite certain you will never insult me in that way again.'

He shrugged off the robe and slid, naked, into the bed beside her.

He added softly, 'I am sure you understand me.'

CHAPTER FIVE

'MY GOD.' Emily almost choked as she flung herself away from him across the bed, her heart juddering against her ribs, like a bird trapped in a cage. She was hideously aware that she'd closed her eyes a split second too late and that a unwanted image of Rafaele Di Salis without his clothes was now engraved on her memory.

Aware too of the sudden warmth of his body in the intimacy of the bed—his nearness. And felt the breath catch in her throat.

'Don't you dare come near me. And don't touch me,' she added wildly, trying to wrench herself free as his hands descended on her shoulders.

'Now you are being foolish.' Calmly but inexorably, Raf pulled her round to face him, his brows lifting as he studied the high-necked nightgown with its demure row of pearl buttons, the long sleeves and the lace-edged collar and cuffs.

'I see the nuns' training has prevailed in the bedroom as well as the kitchen, *cara*,' he murmured, not bothering to hide his amusement. 'So—will you remove this grotesque garment, or would you prefer me to do so?'

'This is revenge, isn't it?' she said shakily. 'Because I had the bad taste to prefer another man and let you know it.'

'They say revenge is sweet.' He shrugged a shoulder. 'Perhaps, tonight, we will both discover if that is true.'

'Please,' she whispered. 'Please don't do this. You—you don't really want me. You know that. And you've punished me enough already. So just—let me go.'

'Without having tasted the pleasures of marriage?' Raf said mockingly. 'I don't think so, my sweet wife. There are so few novelties in life, after all.'

She drew an uneven breath. 'You'll make me hate you.'

'But I thought you already did, *mia cara*,' he said. 'So what have I to lose?' He paused, fingering the collar of her nightgown. 'Now, which of us is it to be?' he questioned softly.

'I'm not taking it off!' she flared.

'As you wish.' As he began to unfasten the buttons, Emily made a grab for his hand, intending to sink her teeth into it.

But he was too quick for her. 'Wildcat,' he accused, laughing, as he captured both her wrists with one lean hand and raised them above her head so that she was helpless. 'If you wish to bite me, Emilia *mia*, then I will gladly show you how and—where. But later. For now, my attention is fully occupied with these buttons, as I refuse to make love to you in this—tent.'

She stared up at him, her eyes enormous in her pale face. She said unevenly, 'How dare you use the word "love"?'

'What would you prefer?' Raf asked, as the last button gave way.

'Some Anglo-Saxon crudity?' His shrug was cynical. 'You will find it all means much the same thing.'

'You are vile,' she said passionately.

'You would naturally think so.'

He released her wrists, but only so that he could whip her nightgown over her head with a speed and deftness that appalled her and toss it to the floor beside the bed.

She tried to pull the duvet up to her chin, but Raf forestalled her.

He said quietly, 'No, *mi amore*, I wish to look at you,' and threw back the covers so that she too was naked in the lamplight.

Emily turned her head away blindly, digging her nails into the palms of her hands.

If I don't look at him, she thought with a kind of desperation, if I don't see him looking at me, I can pretend that this—this isn't happening.

And I can bear it—somehow, especially if I think about something else.

She began to count in her head and had reached twenty before he spoke again.

'Your body is like moonlight, *carissima*. Lovelier even than my dreams of you.'

'Am I supposed to be flattered?' She still didn't look at him.

'You don't wish to be told you are desirable?' He captured her chin, turning her to face him in spite of her resistance.

'Only by the man I love,' she said defiantly.

The dark brows lifted. '*Dio*, you still care about him, after what he has done? You astonish me.'

'He must have been truly desperate,' she said. 'You—you have no idea what it's like to be without money. You've always led this pampered life, with everyone dancing to your tune.'

'You except yourself, do you, from this ludicrous generalisation?' The note in his voice was almost one of disdain.

'No,' she said. 'Because I danced too—when I was fool enough to marry you—and to think I could trust you when you said you wouldn't touch me unless I—wished it.'

His smile was wry. 'Perhaps I thought that, in time, you might change your mind.'

'Then you were wrong.' She was agonisingly conscious that he was propped on an elbow, his hazel eyes still intent on her exposed body, and that she felt not only horribly embarrassed by his continued scrutiny, but *vulnerable*. 'May I cover myself?' she requested curtly.

'No, *mia bella*, not yet.'

'But it's cold.'

He smiled at her. 'Then move closer,' he invited.

She bit her lip. 'Well—at least turn out the light.'

'Later,' he said. 'When it is time for us to sleep. But for now…'

He bent and found her mouth with his.

It was the first time their lips had met since that night at the Manor, when she'd gone into his arms believing he was Simon.

Now the familiarity of his kiss shocked her. Scared her too. Even after all this time she suddenly found herself remembering the taste of him—the warm subtle scent of his skin.

Above all, his gentleness.

And it seemed that nothing had changed.

His lips were light but sensuous as they caressed hers, teasing the soft contours with unhurried persuasion. At the same time, his fingertips were stroking her neck, exploring the hollow beneath her ear and lingering at the base of her throat where the pulse leapt at his touch.

Emily was aware of a strange languor starting to permeate her senses while, deep within her, she felt a faint stirring, like the flutter of a butterfly wing or the slow unfurling of a rosebud.

She heard a small cold voice in her head whisper, So this is seduction.

And knew she was in real danger here.

Because Raf was a master of the game. He'd come here for her surrender and he would be satisfied with nothing less. At the same time, he would consider this initiation of his virgin bride no real contest for him. A foregone conclusion for someone of his experience. And that, before the night was over, she would be clinging to him, begging for more.

But she would make him think again, she told herself fiercely. Because she would fight him with every weapon she possessed— using her pride, her anger and her stubborn will to subdue her emotions—and especially that first kindling of unwanted sexual awareness that she'd just encountered.

She knew she would not prevent his physical possession of her. To struggle would be useless and demeaning. But she would make sure that his was a sterile victory—devoid of the response he would regard as his right. She had boasted to herself that she was immune to him. Now she would prove it by any means available. Retreat to some part of her mind where he could not reach her.

And she began to count to twenty all over again…

Raf allowed his kiss to deepen fractionally, took his mouth from hers for a heartbeat, then kissed her again, running the tip of his tongue delicately along the line of her lips, coaxing them to part for him. But they remained closed and unyielding.

He raised his head and looked down at her. 'No?' he asked on a note of mild curiosity.

She said nothing, just stared back with hostile defiant eyes.

His mouth twisted ruefully. 'Definitely—no,' he murmured and drew her more closely into his arms.

Phase Two, thought Emily, and was tempted to say so aloud.

Only then his hand moved down to her breast, cupping its softness in his palm while his fingers played with her nipple in an enticement as pleasurable as it was calculated.

And for one blind, greedy moment she lost the power of speech along with the ability to think rationally. Her brain was in free fall, her body startled—pierced by a need she'd never known before—or even suspected could exist.

Then he bent and took one swollen rosy peak between his lips, stroking it delicately with his tongue, and as delight lanced through her she felt him smile against her skin.

And, with that, sanity returned, stifling the tiny moan in her throat. Oh, God, he was so sure of her, she thought with shock. So convinced that her inexperienced body would respond with gratitude and joy to this cynical exercise in sexual control.

Oh, why couldn't he have assuaged his anger with some hasty, meaningless coupling, roughly accomplished, that would have fed her own resentment?

But he would never do that. Not when he knew so well how to tantalise and arouse, an ability he'd undoubtedly learned with so many other women, in so many other beds.

But not hers, she told herself with renewed and savage resolve. Never in hers.

Because she did not have to be at the mercy of her senses. She did not have to allow him to win.

Deliberately, she sank her teeth into her lower lip until she tasted blood, using the sharpness of the pain to distract her from the sensual drift of his mouth and hands over her body, the unexpected incitement of his aroused nakedness against her skin.

It would be so easy to yield, she realised, staring up at the ceiling over his shoulder and making herself count the beams. So easy and so fatal.

Because of him, all her dreams of a happy future life had been wrecked. Therefore she would deny him too.

Although she could not so easily control her own physicality, she realised with dismay, as the aching, melting sensation between her legs could attest.

Not even Simon, whom she'd loved, had ever induced this kind of reaction from her—made her feel as if she was about to vanish over the edge of the world.

Nor would she be able to hide it from Raf for much longer, because his knee was between hers, gently coaxing them apart, so that his sensuously exploring hands could gain the intimate access to her body that they sought.

As he began, softly and rhythmically, to caress the secret places of her womanhood, Emily tensed into rigidity, closing her eyes so tightly that coloured sparks danced behind her lids. But when he found the tiniest, most sensitive spot and started to circle it gently with a fingertip, she almost cried out under the force of the sensations he was creating. Realised that her iron determination was almost ready to collapse.

Frantically, she began to recite her twelve times table, verses of poetry she'd learned at school, even her Christmas card list—anything—*anything*—that would help her withstand the witchcraft of his touch and break the web of sensual promise he was weaving round her. Concentrating with such fierceness that she almost stopped breathing.

'Emilia.' His voice seemed to reach her from a great distance and she opened unwilling eyes and looked at him.

The caressing hand had stilled. Indeed, he wasn't touching her at all, but was propped up on a elbow, studying her, the hazel eyes hooded.

He said unsmilingly, 'I feel I am boring you, *carissima*. If it is true, do not hesitate to say so, or tell me if there is some other way I might please you more.'

'I just want you to leave me alone,' she said raggedly. 'Nothing else. Can't you understand that?''

He shrugged. 'Your body does not seem to agree. Continue your passive resistance, if you must, but I still intend to make you my wife. However, it would be easier for both of us if you were to—co-operate a little.' He paused. 'Would it be so impossible to return my kisses—perhaps even to touch me?'

'Anything you want from me, *signore*, you will have to

take.' Her voice was quiet and clear. 'I'll give you nothing. Not now—not ever.

'Nor will I forgive you for breaking the promise you made on our wedding night,' she added huskily.

He moved then, taking her by the shoulders and jerking her towards him, crushing her breasts against his chest as his mouth took hers in a bruising kiss that was in total contrast to his earlier consideration.

She was gasping for breath, when he released her, allowing her to fall back against the pillows.

'This is our wedding night,' he said softly. 'Here and now. And I will mark it with another promise to you, *mia cara.*

'I swear that there will come a time—some day, some night soon—when you will desire me as much as I want you now.

'And then, may God help you.'

He turned away, stretching down for his robe on the floor beside the bed. And, for a moment, with an odd jump of her heart, Emily thought he was leaving.

But as he straightened, she realised that he'd only been reaching for the protection he intended to use.

He saw her eyes widen and said icily, 'Our marriage has no permanent basis, Emilia. It follows, therefore, that there can be no risk of a child.'

He positioned himself so that she could feel the hardness and strength of him pressing against the junction of her thighs. And the breath caught in her throat.

'Relax a little,' he directed. 'Or I may hurt you.'

'Hurt me then,' she flung at him. 'Do you think I care?'

As his mouth tightened in frustration and his eyes glittered with sudden anger, she knew a brief, almost savage satisfaction.

Then he moved fractionally and entered her.

He paused, drawing a deep breath. He said quietly, 'Bend your knees.' And it suddenly seemed wiser to obey.

He took her slowly, easing his way into her, his eyes never leaving her face. She lay very still, staring past him, her clenched fist pressed against her mouth, bracing herself mentally. But there was no pain. And, instead, out of nowhere, she found she wanted very badly to cry. But did not.

Because there was nothing to cry about. She'd endured—hadn't she—the worst he could do to her and it would soon be over.

She began repeating, Soon—over soon, inside her head like a mantra.

For a moment he too was motionless, as if he were waiting for something, then he said huskily, 'I would have given you the world, Emilia,' and began to thrust his way to climax in long, powerful strokes.

Yet, in spite of everything, as she lay beneath him, waiting for him to finish with her, Emily became aware of one infinitesimal, bewildered moment when the stark driving force of his body seemed to trigger a tiny echo of response that flickered uncertainly somewhere in the depths of her being, but was immediately extinguished.

And, even as her throat tightened in shock, she felt his movements quicken almost to frenzy until, at the last, he cried out and was still.

Emily remained where she was too, because she had no other choice with Raf slumped on top of her, the dark dishevelled head pillowed on her small breasts.

When he eventually lifted himself away from her, there was none of the triumph in his face that she'd expected. In fact, she thought, he looked reflective, almost sombre. But if he had regrets, he certainly did not express them aloud. Or any other opinion either.

In the event, he simply got out of bed, put on his robe and left the room without a word.

So the mantra had worked, Emily thought, gulping with relief as she straightened the bed before turning on to her side and pulling the covers up over her shoulder. It really was—all over and she'd survived, without visible marks. She was conscious of aching a little internally, but she guessed that was only to be expected.

It also occurred to her that, in spite of the provocation she'd deliberately offered, he had not translated his anger into brutality. On the contrary, she could accept, in the absence of other criteria, that he'd probably been—almost considerate.

She'd not been really hurt, she thought wryly, just humiliated. But, all in all, it could have been very much worse.

Then she heard the bedroom door reopen and realised she'd been altogether too optimistic.

She turned defensively—warily. 'I—I thought you'd gone back to your own room.'

'And so I have.' He put the bottle of wine he was carrying and two glasses down on the night table. There was faint mockery in his voice. 'My place is here, beside you, *mia bella sposa*.'

He sat down on the edge of the bed to pour the wine, then handed her a glass. 'To our real honeymoon,' he said and drank.

Emily stared at him. 'What are you talking about?' she asked breathlessly. 'You got what you wanted. And I accept now that there'll be no annulment,' she added bitterly. 'You've made quite sure of that.'

She drew a breath. 'But I'll agree to your conditions for a divorce as long as—all of *this*—stops now and you leave me in peace.'

'You thought that, having waited for almost three years, I would be satisfied by that one lacklustre performance?' Raf asked cynically. 'You are mistaken.' He smiled at her. 'You have an exquisite body, my sweet one, and I intend to enjoy *all of this* whenever and however I wish, for the duration of our marriage.'

'But—surely—you came here to talk about a divorce!' She was pleading suddenly.

'Oh, that is postponed,' he said. 'Indefinitely.'

Her voice was a croak of disbelief. 'Until when?'

He shrugged. 'Until—perhaps—the ice melts.' His smile was sardonic. 'You see, Emilia, you have become a challenge.'

She lifted her chin. 'Even though I've just shown that I don't want you—and never will?'

'You punish no one but yourself, *mia cara*,' he told her quietly. 'A man's ability to gain satisfaction does not depend on his partner's pleasure. Although it is enhanced by it, *naturalmente*.'

He paused. 'And never is a long time, Emilia. While I—I have become used to waiting. It will not be such a hardship, especially when I expect the eventual rewards to be infinite,' he added softly.

Her voice shook. 'I hate you.'

'Then at least you will not weary me with declarations of undying love when we part.' His tone was brisk as he took the untouched wine from her and set it aside, then reached into the pocket of his robe. 'Now, give me your hand.'

She obeyed reluctantly, looking down mutinously as Raf slid her wedding ring back on to her finger.

'Where did you get that?'

'From your former bedroom at the Manor. I gathered from the lawyers, among other things, that you were no longer wearing it and made a special detour.' His smile was ironic. 'We are finally man and wife, *carissima*, and you will in future acknowledge as much to the world.'

She was still staring down at the gleam of gold in the lamplight, but her head jerked up. 'You said—former bedroom?'

'I have instructed the good Signora Penistone to prepare the master suite for us both when we next return to the Manor.'

'But you can't,' she protested in sudden anguish. 'Those were my father's rooms.'

'His rooms, Emilia,' Raf said quietly. 'Not his shrine.'

'You have no right to give such an order in my house!'

'I have any rights I choose to assume.' He shrugged off the robe and rejoined her in the bed, pulling her effortlessly towards him. 'And maybe now is the time I should remind you of some of them,' he added softly and put his lips to the hollow between her breasts.

Emily awoke slowly. For a moment she felt totally disorientated, but two things rapidly became apparent—that a pale, sharp light was filtering through the curtains and filling the room and that it was difficult to move because she seemed weighted to the bed.

She turned her head cautiously and saw Raf sleeping beside her, his arm thrown carelessly across her body.

And then she remembered—a wave of embarrassed heat sweeping over her body as all the events of the previous night returned inexorably to haunt her. Everything he'd said—and, oh, God, everything he'd done.

Inch by inch, she began to edge away from him across the bed, but he did not stir.

Too worn out by his exertions, no doubt, she thought, loathing him.

She gave a silent sigh of relief as her feet touched the icy floor. She retrieved her discarded nightdress and put it on in lieu of a dressing gown, then tiptoed surreptitiously across to the window and looked round the curtain.

She had to repress a whistle of dismay, because there was the snow. And not the genteel icing sugar effect she was used to either. Overnight, the world outside the cottage had become a series of anonymous lumps and bumps, shrouded by drifts.

It looked, she thought unhappily, as if she was going to be stranded here for a while—and with him. And there wasn't a damned thing she could do about it.

She sighed, then went quietly round the room collecting a handful of underwear, a pair of dark blue cord trousers and a cream roll-neck sweater in thick wool.

Then she slipped out, closing the door noiselessly behind her, and went to the bathroom, running a tub as hot as she could stand. For a while she sat in a little huddle while the water cooled, legs drawn up to her chin as she stared into nothingness, as she came reluctantly to terms with what had happened to her.

She felt exhausted too—by the unexpected strain of the passive resistance she'd managed to sustain until Rafaele had eventually turned away from her to sleep and her taut, obdurate body had finally been able to relax.

Not that her stance had deterred him in the least, she thought bitterly. In fact, there'd been moments when she'd suspected he was even amused by her obstinate refusal to permit herself even the slightest response to his lovemaking.

He'd simply shrugged and continued to use her for his own entertainment, as if she was merely some expensive toy with a range of possibilities that he was curious to exploit.

And doing so, Emily realised, with a complete lack of inhibition that she found impossible to relate to the cool, elegant young man who'd appeared from time to time in her life over the past three years.

Causing her, she thought, the kind of humiliation that she would never be able to forget. Or forgive.

She regretted now that she hadn't fought him off, kicking and scratching, because instinct told her that Rafaele Di Salis would have never lowered himself by resorting to using his superior strength.

But now it was much too late.

Dry eyes burning, she picked up the soap and began to wash herself from head to foot, massaging the lather carefully into every inch of her skin so not one trace of him would be left behind.

Until next time, a small wintry voice in her head reminded her and she flinched, wondering just how much of him she would be made to endure.

Surely he would become irritated with her stubbornness before long and find himself a more responsive lady.

He wouldn't have to look far, she thought. His name had most recently been linked with that of Valentina Colona, a twenty-seven-year-old former model who'd retired from the catwalk several years before to marry a wealthy industrialist from Milan, three times her age. He was now in failing health and confined to his villa in Tuscany, but his money had helped her start a chain of boutiques called Valentina X and she'd just launched her own perfume brand with the same name.

And for the last six months she'd been coyly referred to in the gossip columns as Raf Di Salis's 'constant companion'.

Emily even knew what she looked like—raven hair, a heart-shaped face almost doll-like in its beauty and a stunning body that managed to be lissom and voluptuous at the same time.

And last night Raf dared call me beautiful, she thought stormily. Compared with her, I'm a stick insect.

But what made his current behaviour truly inexplicable was the widely quoted story that Signora Colona would one day become the next Contessa Di Salis.

As if Emily herself did not exist, her marriage to Raf brushed to the sidelines, she'd told herself when she read the newspaper gossip. But she felt strangely stung just the same. Which was why she'd gambled that Raf would accept the offered annulment as a quick way out of his marital dilemma.

Only Raf, as he'd made only too clear last night, had not seen it that way.

Maybe he doesn't wish to give his future wife any impression that he is less than the master in his own house, she thought, grimacing.

But if he really loves her and wants to marry her one day, why is he here with me? How can he betray her by having sex with someone else, even if it is only his wife?

That's what I should have asked him, she told herself. After all, I'd stupidly let slip that I knew all about his extra-marital exploits.

But somehow accepting that Raf was an incorrigible womaniser, involved in a string of casual *affaires*, was easier than recognising him as a man capable of being deeply in love with just one woman.

Yet, in spite of that, he'd come here looking for revenge because she'd made him look a fool. But surely he could have achieved his aim without hurting the woman he loved?

On the other hand, lovers who were married to other people probably had to allow a certain sexual leeway in their relationships—were forced to be realistic about their partners' marital obligations.

Maybe Valentina Colona was that kind of realist, although she must surely know that Raf's marriage had only existed on paper until last night.

But maybe she didn't care—as long as she won in the end.

Emily suddenly felt intensely dispirited and was conscious of the heated bitterness of tears rising in her throat. But she fought them back fiercely as she lifted herself out of the bath and reached for a towel.

Whatever Raf might have threatened, she told herself strongly, he wouldn't want their marriage to drag on. It would prove far too costly.

Because he needed to concentrate on making yet more millions. At the same time, he couldn't afford to neglect his mistress either.

Dried and dressed, she combed her hair severely back from her face and plaited it into a braid, trying to ignore the bruised eyes that stared back at her from the mirror.

She'd brought only a few cosmetics with her, just moisturiser, a lipstick and mascara, when what she really needed was a mask to shelter behind.

Because, sooner or later, Raf would wake up and come downstairs in search of her. And it was going to take every scrap of courage she possessed to face him—to start pretending all over again that she didn't care what he'd done to her. That, somehow, this small cottage and the intimacy it inevitably imposed didn't matter either. That she would get through the days and find some way to endure the nights without surrendering her integrity.

But how long could she feasibly remain focused? Last night it had taken every scrap of will-power she possessed to ignore her bewildered, starving senses and continue her inimical stance against him. However hard she tried to distract herself, she'd already realised that it was almost impossible to separate herself completely from what he was doing to her.

Especially when he seemed equally determined to arouse her.

Suddenly she found herself wondering—actually imagining how Raf would make love when he was *in* love. How tender he would be—whether there would be a difference in his kisses— in the touch of his hands. What he might say to his woman when they finally lay together, all passion spent. Whether he would simply hold her close in adoring silence, his lips against her hair?

And stopped herself right there, her mouth dry. Because there was no point in that kind of speculation. On the contrary, she told herself, it was positively dangerous.

She shivered as she turned away from the mirror and went slowly downstairs to begin the first day of her unwanted marriage.

CHAPTER SIX

DOWNSTAIRS, Emily discovered, there was the unexpected lifeline of housework to rescue her from any further risky introspection.

Cleaning a house had never been her sole responsibility before, she thought ruefully as she cleaned the grate and laid the fire before tidying and dusting the living room. She'd always looked after her own room at school and at the Manor, of course, and pitched in to help elsewhere when necessary, but there'd always been the back-up of efficient staff.

And, even after her marriage to Simon, nothing much would have changed. She'd assumed at first that Simon would want to live in London again and that they'd start out in a small flat like other young couples but, to her surprise, this hadn't been his idea at all.

'I like working from home,' he'd told her. 'And there's endless room at the Manor to set up a proper office for me.' He'd smiled at her. 'And you'd hate to live anywhere else, darling. Admit it.'

'But don't you want us to have a home of our own?' she'd asked, vaguely troubled.

'But we have,' he'd said. 'And it's beautiful. Besides, what would you do all day in some grotty flat? You're hardly one of nature's housewives.'

No, she thought wincing at the memory. He could have been right about that, although she realised now that his wish to live at the Manor had not been prompted by any consideration for her.

But she'd wanted so badly to believe he was in love with her and that, this time, everything would be wonderful. She'd needed to think it. Had clutched at it desperately, as if it was a life-belt and not a straw.

Had never asked herself seriously whether, as her father's heiress, it was the lifestyle he wanted more than herself. The big house, with its paid staff to do his bidding.

Perhaps I didn't dare ask too many questions, she thought. In case I didn't like the answers.

She shook herself out of her depressing reverie. She had work to do and there was no hired help at Braeside Cottage. It was all down to her here and she was determined that, whatever her private failings as a wife, Raf would have nothing to complain of in her domestic abilities.

She looked at her watch. It was nearly midday already, so she would cook the chicken for supper. But, for now, she would make some coffee, she thought, glancing restively towards the stairs. And maybe some toast. However, if Raf wanted some, he could fetch it. Even if he did consider he was on honeymoon, and the thought made her writhe inwardly, there would be no bedside delivery service.

She filled the kettle and was just getting out the mugs, when there was a loud knock at the front door.

She opened it to find Angus McEwen standing on the doorstep. He was wearing a thick jacket and what appeared to be fisherman's waders over his trousers.

'Hello, there,' he greeted her, grinning broadly. 'I came to make sure you were all right. See if you needed help lighting the fire or anything.'

'You mean you've walked up in all this?' Emily forced a smile of her own. 'That's incredibly kind of you.'

'Och, it's no so bad.' He indicated the waders. 'These belonged to my late uncle. He was great on the fishing and Auntie Maggie always said they'd come in handy.' He paused. 'Did you know someone's left a vehicle here? I don't remember seeing it last night.'

'I drove it here from the airport,' Raf's voice said from behind her.

Emily hadn't heard a sound from the stairs, but she saw Angus glance past her, his face changing to an expression of astonishment that was almost comical. Except she didn't feel like laughing.

Instead, she tensed as Raf came to stand beside her, his arm encircling her and his hand resting on her hip in a gesture of deliberate possession.

He was not dressed, unless she counted the robe he was casually holding around him as clothing, and she was never likely to do that.

'*Buon giorno*,' he drawled. 'May we help you in some way?'

Angus opened his mouth, tried to speak, failed and began again. 'I—I'm sorry. I—I don't mean to intrude, but I thought—I understood that Miss Blake was here alone.'

'That is indeed what she planned originally,' Raf said softly. He drew Emily slightly closer to him. 'But I decided to surprise her.'

Angus's ears suddenly went pink, indicating that the probable nature of the surprise was not lost on him.

Emily, realising the floor was not about to open and swallow her as she'd prayed it might, found her own voice, 'Angus, this is my husband, the Count Di Salis.' She paused, allowing him to assimilate this, then continued, 'Rafaele—Mr McEwen's aunt looks after the cottage for—for your friends. He was—concerned that I was here by myself in this weather.'

'So I heard as I came downstairs, and I am glad that I can reassure him that you are perfectly safe, *mi amore*.' Raf was smiling. 'You have had a long walk, my friend,' he added pleasantly. 'Believe that I shall be sure to inform Signora Albero, when I see her next, how well you look after her tenants.'

'Aye, well—thanks,' Angus managed as he turned away. Then paused, his hand going into an inside pocket. 'I thought you might like a Sunday paper, Miss—er, Mrs…'

'Contessa,' Raf supplied.

Angus nodded, gulped and handed over the folded broadsheet. 'And it said on the radio just now that the weather's going to get worse before it gets better,' he added glumly. 'I thought mebbe I should mention that too.'

For a moment they watched him trudge off, then Raf drew Emily back into the cottage, firmly closing the door.

'So what was that all about?' She turned on him hotly. 'Why not have a banner made with SHE'S MINE in huge letters?'

'It will not be necessary. He got the message. I regret his disappointment,' he added lightly. 'But the exercise will do him good.'

'He came here to help,' she protested. She shook her head. 'You can't believe, can you, that someone might actually go out of their way—just to do a kindness?'

'I think it unlikely, yes.' Raf followed her into the kitchen. 'For a man to walk so far in these conditions to see a beautiful girl with no hope of reward? Never.'

'Perhaps you shouldn't judge other men by your own dubious standards, *signore*.'

'You do not think I can be kind?' He shrugged. 'On the other hand, you have not granted me much opportunity to prove otherwise, *carissima*.'

'If you'd wanted to be kind, you'd have stayed away.' Emily spooned coffee into the cafetière with fierce precision. Then paused. 'Would you like something to eat?'

Raf burst out laughing. 'You are a girl of contradictions, *cara*. Would you not prefer to let me starve?'

'Yes,' she said. 'But coping with a corpse wouldn't be practical.' She hesitated again. 'We could have poached eggs on toast, perhaps.' She added stiltedly, 'I—I thought I'd roast the chicken this evening—if that's all right with you.'

'But of course.' He paused. 'So we have an empty afternoon before us,' he went on softly. 'How can we occupy it, I wonder.'

'You could always start by putting some clothes on,' Emily suggested tautly.

'Perhaps.' He paused. 'Or maybe I might persuade you to take yours off instead.'

Her breath quickened. 'No!'

He leaned against the archway. 'That is a very definite negative, *carissima*.' He sounded faintly amused. 'I can see why you scared my lawyers, especially poor Pietro.'

She glared at him. 'This is not a joke. I have no intention of performing some kind of striptease in broad daylight in order to please you.' Her voice was ragged. 'And, if you push it, I'll walk out of here and to hell with the snow. I'd rather freeze in a drift than be degraded like that.'

'My sympathies are with the drift,' he returned coolly. He

studied her for a moment. 'I am surprised that you find the idea of undressing in front of a man to be degrading, Emilia.' He added sardonically, 'I remember a time when you seemed eager to do so.'

Oh, God, she thought, you would remind me of that awful night. But you're still wrong. Because I never felt like that— never wanted to—not even with Simon...

Aloud, she said frigidly, 'That was with the man I loved, *signore*. Not you. Besides, it was the middle of the night.'

'Daylight, lamplight, starlight,' he said reflectively. 'Does it really make such a difference?'

'Yes,' she said. 'It does.' She looked at him, lifting her chin. 'I realise that I can't prevent you—helping yourself to me at night, but my days are going to be my own and I want that understood.'

There was a loaded silence, then Raf gave a brief shrug. 'Very well. You may have them, if they are so important to you.' He paused. 'But your nights will belong to me. Is it agreed?'

She gave a small jerky nod.

'Then maybe you too could make a concession, *carissima*,' he said softly. 'And, tonight, show me a little of the kindness you spoke of so eloquently a few moments ago.'

He turned away. 'Now, to demonstrate my good faith, I will get dressed.' He ran a musing hand over his chin. 'But I shall wait to shave, I think, until later.'

Digesting the implication in his words, Emily's throat tightened. She said in a falsely bright voice, 'Then I'll hold breakfast for you.'

'*Grazie*.' He inclined his head to her with a touch of mockery. 'You are becoming a wonderful wife, *carissima mia*,' he added softly. And went.

Emily leaned against the sink. He had allowed her to win, she thought shakily. But she was not deceived. Because it was only a very minor triumph in the war of attrition between them.

Besides, he'd made it clear that he expected ultimate victory. That nothing else would do for him.

She said under her breath, But I won't let that happen. I—I can't... Because it would change my life for ever. Whereas, once I cease to be a novelty, he—he will just walk away.

She stared through the window at the bleak and dazzling whiteness outside.

But wasn't that what she really wanted—for him to go? she asked herself desperately. And somehow could find no answer.

It was a strange afternoon. In spite of Raf's assurance, Emily still felt tense and on edge. After all, he'd broken his word before, she told herself. What was to stop him doing so again?

Besides, the other promise he'd made to her last night still lingered uneasily in her mind.

When she carried the tray of poached eggs and coffee into the living room she discovered that the fire was crackling briskly in the grate and Raf, soberly clad in khaki trousers and a black woollen long-sleeved shirt, was kneeling on the hearthrug, adding more coal to the blaze.

'Oh,' she said, 'I meant to do that.'

'From now on, I will attend to it.' He gave her a brief smile as he got to his feet, adding lightly, 'I do not wish you to ruin your hands, *cara*. Or give your admirer another excuse to call.'

She said between her teeth, 'Once and for all, he is not my admirer.'

He gave her a dry look. 'No longer, certainly,' he agreed, as he sat down at the table.

She was trying to think of a suitably chilly riposte when her attention was suddenly distracted.

'Oh, God, it's snowing again.'

'We were warned that it might.' Raf poured the coffee. 'Is it a problem?'

'Your car,' she said. 'I thought we might be able to dig it out—and leave.'

'To go where?' He sounded politely interested as he cut into his toast.

'Does it matter? Just—away from here. After all, we—we both have lives to get back to.'

'And it would suit you much better if those lives were resumed hundreds of miles apart,' he murmured. 'No deal, *carissima*. The forecast in the newspaper warns that roads in this area may become impassable for a while and only essential journeys should be attempted in the rest of the region. Your reluctance to be alone with me hardly justifies the risk.'

He paused. 'And you made the decision to come here.'

'I had no idea it would be like this,' she said. 'What's more, I bet you didn't realise that we might be marooned here when you set the arrangement up.' She shook her head. 'Oh, God, I was so damned stupid. I should have realised it was a trap.'

'Is that how you see it?' Raf asked silkily. 'Yet I find it delightful. Quiet, remote. The ideal place to begin married life. Don't you think?'

'You don't want to know what I think,' she said bitterly.

'Perhaps,' he said. 'If you relaxed a little, Emilia, you might enjoy being here too.'

And he was not simply referring to the environment, Emily thought, biting her lip.

When the meal was over, Raf cleared the table, in spite of her protests, and carried the used cups and plates into the kitchen. Emily followed unwillingly and found him crouched in front of the fridge studying the chicken.

He said, 'Do you wish to cook it in wine? Shall I fetch some from the cellar?'

'No, thank you. I'm simply going to roast it.'

'And these are the vegetables?' He looked at them with an air of faint disbelief. 'May I help prepare them?'

'That won't be necessary.' She hesitated. 'As you can see, this is a very small kitchen, so could it be designated as my space? Please?'

There was a brief silence, then he said too courteously, 'But of course. Forgive my intrusion.'

He disappeared into the living room and Emily tackled the washing-up. When it was completed, she cleaned all the surfaces until they shone, then wiped them over again. She was tempted to scrub the floor—anything that would delay her from having to join him in the living room—but she didn't want him to think that she was nervous. Even though she was.

But when she eventually ventured in he barely seemed to notice. He'd discovered a box of chessmen and a board somewhere and seemed absorbed in a problem he'd found in the newspaper.

She sat on the sofa opposite, her legs curled under her, and watched the leaping flames in the grate. But she realised, after a while, that she was also stealing covert looks at Raf. It occurred to her that she'd never before spent such a long time completely alone with him. And that, for at least half of it, she'd been naked. And so, of course, had he…

'Do you play chess?' he asked suddenly and she jumped, colour flooding her face, as she realised where her thoughts had been drifting.

'I know the basic moves,' she said. 'Nothing else.'

'Would you like to learn?'

'No, thank you. I always preferred backgammon.'

'Yes,' he said quietly. 'I remember.' He paused. 'There is a set in the cupboard over there, if you would like a game.'

'Oh, no.' Her disclaimer was hasty. 'I—I only ever played against my father.'

'And a different opponent would naturally be out of the question,' he said expressionlessly and returned to his chess problem.

There was another silence.

'I see there are books here, but I brought some others with me,' Emily mentioned eventually. 'They're upstairs. But they might not appeal to you.'

'They are romantic books, perhaps—for women? The search for Mr Right?' His faint smile did not indicate any particular amusement.

She said coolly, 'One of them's *Anna Karenina*. I don't think she fits that category. And there are some detective stories too. You're welcome to borrow them—if you want.'

'*Grazie*,' he said. 'And the cupboard also contains a radio, a pack of cards, three jigsaw puzzles and a game of Snakes and Ladders. Even without television, we do not lack for entertainment,' he added sardonically.

'Never a dull moment,' Emily commented and got to her feet. 'I'll go and find the books.'

She had to steel herself to enter the bedroom. She didn't want to look at the bed either but, to her annoyance, she found her glance drawn to it. She was surprised to see that it had been neatly made, its pillows plumped up and the covers smoothed. As if it had never been occupied. His handiwork, she realised with bewilderment, and quite the last thing she would have expected.

She lifted the bag out of the bottom of the wardrobe and turned, only to cannon into Raf who was standing right behind her.

Her mouth went dry. Oh, God, surely he couldn't have construed her departure upstairs as some kind of invitation? she thought, hugging the bag defensively against her body. 'What—what do you want?'

'To help you with these,' Raf told her curtly, taking the bag from her slackened grasp. 'What else?'

He walked away from her out of the room and, after a brief hesitation, Emily followed him downstairs.

She said stiltedly, 'I'm sorry. I—I thought…'

'I know what you thought.' He was putting the chess pieces back in their box. 'But you were wrong.' His tone bit. 'So let us leave the subject.'

'But can't you see now why I want to leave here?' She looked at him pleadingly. 'It—it's so cramped. And if we keep—bumping into each other, it's bound to lead to—to misunderstandings,' she ended miserably.

'Only in your own head, *cara*.' He sounded bored, his attention now focused on the contents of the book bag. He went through them all, then chose the new Patricia Cornwell, which Emily had mentally reserved for herself.

Not that she intended to argue about it, she told herself. Anything at all that might keep his mind off her had to be a bonus.

It was almost a relief when she could disappear into the kitchen and begin preparations for supper.

But once the chicken had begun to sizzle in the oven and the vegetables were prepared, there was nothing to detain her and she came back to resume her seat on the other side of the hearth. And to wrestle with her unhappy thoughts.

Eventually, she cleared her throat. 'Rafaele—may I talk to you?'

'With pleasure.' He put his book aside. 'But I thought you preferred silence.'

'I suppose that's really one of the things I want to talk about.' She swallowed. 'The way things are, you can't really mean for us to live together—not in any real sense—when we leave here. Not even on a temporary basis.'

'But that is exactly my intention, *cara*. I thought I had made that clear.' He shrugged. 'And the duration of the marriage has yet to be decided.'

She stared across at him. 'And that's all you have to say?'

'What else is there?'

'I'd have thought—plenty.' She took a deep breath. 'I—I acknowledge that I made you angry over the annulment thing. But can't you now also acknowledge that you've punished me enough? And let me go? Let us both go, in fact?'

His brows lifted. 'You think this is my only reason for being here—to teach you a lesson?' He sounded politely curious.

'In your own words—what else is there?'

He said slowly, 'Perhaps—that you are a beautiful girl with an exquisite body.'

She flushed. 'Even if it was true, I'd be just one more on a long list,' she said tautly. 'As we both know. So please don't think that offering me meaningless flattery will make last night—what you did to me any more acceptable.'

'I shall consider myself rebuked.' He watched her for a moment. 'But at least when you find another husband you will have some experience of married life to take with you. Comfort yourself with that.'

'You're all heart,' Emily said bitterly. 'But, after due consideration, I think I shall prefer to remain single.'

She paused. 'However, while we're on the subject, I understand you are intending to remarry. Is—is that true?'

'Perfectly true.'

She leaned forward, her voice suddenly intense. 'Then how can you possibly be here with me—like this? What about the woman you love? I—I presume you do love her?'

'Yes,' he returned coolly. 'But she has a husband, just as I have a wife. And, as I cannot live with her as I wish, then you make a charming substitute, *carissima*. After all, who better to share my bed at this juncture than the wife I have so cruelly neglected in the past?'

'We have very different ideas on cruelty,' Emily said cuttingly. 'Won't she care that you've decided to begin sleeping with me—after all this time?'

'She knows that our marriage was solely a matter of convenience, certainly. But so was hers, and she is realistic enough to understand that these arrangements have their obligations and their inevitable compromises.' He gave her a level look. 'For us, happiness is the future, not the past or even the present.'

'That's an incredibly cynical viewpoint.' Emily lifted her chin. 'I wouldn't want to think of the man I loved having even duty sex with another woman.'

'Especially if duty also becomes a pleasure, *mi amore*,' he murmured, his mouth twisting. 'Is that what you were going to say?'

'No,' she said. 'Especially if I thought he was forcing himself on someone who didn't want him.'

'Do not let it trouble you, Emilia,' he said softly. 'I am sure a man that you loved would do none of these things. That you would fill his heart to the exclusion of all others.' He smiled at her. 'But until you find this prince, you will continue to be my wife. And—do your duty. As I shall do mine.'

'You're quite adamant, aren't you?' she said bitterly. 'There's nothing I can say—nothing I can do to persuade you to release me from this—unspeakable situation?'

'You exaggerate, *cara*,' Raf drawled. 'You have spoken on the subject quite frankly. And it is hardly a life sentence,' he added with another faint shrug.

'Although it already seems like it.' She looked back at him, her green eyes clouded with resentment. 'Does your future wife realise, *signore*, how easily you break your promises? And what a casual approach you have to commitment?'

'When I make my vows to her, Emilia, they will be kept.' There was a sudden harshness in his voice. 'And, when she is all mine, I will belong to her as completely. There will be no other— ever. Now, do you have anything more you wish to ask?'

'No,' she said quietly, aware of an odd twist of the heart. 'If she's prepared to settle for your future fidelity, that's her concern.' *After all, someone as glamorous and sexy as Valentina Colona would hardly see me as any kind of rival, even in the short term.*

She swallowed. 'At the same time, I feel really sorry for her husband.'

'There is no need, I assure you. He is content to settle for what he has.'

'Then there's nothing more to be said.' Emily got to her feet. 'And I'd be better employed checking on dinner.'

'One duty at least that you can perform without reservations, *carissima*,' he said blandly and picked up his book.

In the kitchen she attempted to relieve her feelings by slamming the oven door and clanging saucepans together, but her sense of mingled anger and bewilderment persisted unabated.

I can't bear what's happening to me, she thought swallowing. I have to get away from him. But how?

Even without the snow, she couldn't think of a place to go where he wouldn't be able to trace her and follow. Financially her options were limited too. Until her twenty-first birthday, she had no direct control over her affairs and she was beginning to realise how deeply this could matter.

Up to now, admittedly, Rafaele had kept a light hand on the reins, as well as strictly maintaining his distance, so she'd been able to stifle her resentment at the arbitrary way his dual role in her life had been imposed, in the sure knowledge that it would soon be over.

Now, in the space of twenty-four hours, there were suddenly no more certainties and her countdown to freedom had turned into a test of her endurance that she dared not fail.

Demanding the annulment had been a supreme mistake. What on earth had made her think she could challenge him like that and get away with it?

I was angry, she thought. It was as simple as that. And maybe I simply wanted to make him angry too.

But why? That was the question that she could not answer.

Had she allowed the stories in the gossip columns to get to her at last? Was this some kind of—personal backlash because she found herself being air-brushed out of his life in this arbitrary way? An impulsive but misjudged bid to remind him that she still existed?

Yet why should she even care—when she herself was supposed to be in love with Simon?

None of it made any sense, she thought unhappily.

Yes, she'd been stupid to attract his attention so blatantly, when she could just have accepted his terms and faded quietly out of the picture, which was, after all, what she'd always expected would happen.

Even so, she'd never dreamed her attempt to needle him would have such dire consequences. At most, she'd expected an icy rebuke. Never this kind of retribution.

But then, what had she ever really known about Rafaele Di Salis, except that her father had trusted him, even though the younger man had owed him some mysterious debt?

And, apart from the stories in the scandal sheets, and in spite of the enforced intimacies of the previous night, Emily thought, biting her lip, he was still pretty much of an enigma to her.

For instance, all she knew about his family background was that his parents were both dead, and that was information that she'd gleaned solely from her father, who'd warned her that it was not something that Rafaele cared to speak about. He'd also suggested that she shouldn't ask questions, but wait until her husband chose to discuss the subject with her.

Only he never had.

But when we've been together before, we've barely had conversations, thought Emily, let alone discussions. Talking is a sharing thing, and I must have known even then that it was dangerous to share. That I needed to keep him at arm's length.

I wish I'd also realised how unwise it might be to make him angry.

For a moment it was as if her eyes blurred suddenly and she ran an impatient hand across them. She couldn't afford any sign of weakness. She'd tried rejection and she'd tried pleading with him, all to no avail. Now, all that was left to her was survival.

I will get through this, she told herself, and I'll walk away when it's over without a backward glance. I have to.

The living room was empty when she went in to set the table but, just as she'd finished arranging the cutlery, Raf appeared from the cellar with a handful of candles and a selection of pottery holders.

'Oh.' Emily hesitated as he put two of them on the table and lit them. 'Isn't that a little extreme? After all, this is hardly formal dining.'

'You saw the lights flickering, *si*?' There was faint impatience in his tone.

'Well—yes.' *So it hadn't been her eyes, after all.*

'I think we may lose the power,' he went on. 'And I thought it would be safer to make other arrangements now rather than later.' He paused. 'I would rather not test the cellar steps in the dark.'

'No,' she said with constraint. 'Of course not.'

His brows lifted. 'You don't like candlelight?'

She shrugged evasively. 'I'd prefer it not to be a necessity.'

His glance was faintly mocking. 'You favour romance over practicality, *cara*? How very sweet. I am encouraged.'

'Actually,' she said, 'given the choice, I'd like you to fall down the cellar steps and break your neck, *signore*.' And heard his low laugh follow her back to the kitchen.

As a meal, it turned out better than she could have hoped. What the chicken lacked in flavour, it made up in succulence, and the vegetables were perfectly cooked. And Emily discovered, to her great surprise, that she was ravenous.

'There isn't a great deal left for tomorrow,' she said ruefully, eyeing the carcass.

He shrugged. 'The bones will make soup. So do not worry, Emilia, and drink some more wine.' He refilled her glass. 'Believe me, I will not allow you to starve.'

There was a silence, then she said slowly, 'Will you tell me something?'

'Perhaps,' he said. 'Ask me and I will decide.'

It didn't sound particularly hopeful, but she ploughed on.

'My father told me you'd offered to marry me because you owed him—big time.' She swallowed. 'I'm just curious to know my—market value.'

There was a silence. Then, at last, 'The debt is immeasurable,' he said expressionlessly. 'But it was the only repayment he ever asked of me, so I could not refuse. Does that content you?'

'How can it?' Her voice sounded stifled. 'When it would have been so much easier on both of us if you'd simply—found the money from somewhere.'

His faint smile twisted. 'And even easier to be wise in retrospect, *cara*.' He rose to his feet. 'Now I will make some coffee.'

Once the clearing away was done, in actual hours and minutes it seemed a long while until bedtime, but Emily found the time passing with disquieting speed as she turned the pages of the thriller she was trying to read with only the sketchiest idea of what was taking place in print.

She could not concentrate. In spite of herself, her eyes kept straying to the neat wooden clock in the centre of the mantel-piece, watching the inexorable movement of its hands. The countdown to the inevitable moment when she would have to submit to him all over again in that big bed upstairs, she thought, her throat tightening.

Seated opposite her, Raf appeared to have no such concerns. He seemed totally absorbed in his own book as he lounged in the corner of the sofa, reaching every now and then for his wineglass.

And how *dared* he be so relaxed, when she was like a cat on hot bricks?

And the worst of it was that she really *wanted* to go to bed. She was being assailed by wave after wave of drowsiness, which she had to conceal at all costs, she thought resentfully, putting her hand to her mouth in an attempt to stifle yet another yawn.

'Why don't you stop struggling, *carissima*, and admit you are tired?'

He was watching her, she realised angrily, with open amuse-ment and had probably been doing so for several minutes, book discarded, hands loosely clasped behind his head as he leaned back on the cushions.

'I'm not a bit tired,' she denied hurriedly and saw his smile widen.

'I am delighted to hear it,' he told her softly. He got up and put the guard in front of the fire, then moved round the room, checking the door and turning off the lamps. Making the usual preparations for the night, as if he'd done so a hundred times before. Whereas, in fact…

Her mind closed off at that point. She sat where she was, unmoving, her whole body taut, aware of the uneven barrage of her heart against her ribs.

At last he came to her in the fire glow, reaching down for her small, cold hand and drawing her to her feet.

'It is time for bed, *mia bella*,' he said quietly and led her upstairs to the room where the shadows waited.

CHAPTER SEVEN

EMILY stood in the middle of the room, staring down at the floor, anticipating the moment when he would touch her and the fight to resist the lure of her senses would start once again. Along with the realisation that she was by no means sure of victory.

Rafaele came to stand behind her and she felt him remove the band that confined her hair and begin to free it from its tight braid. His fingers were gentle and very thorough, combing through the silky strands until they hung loose about her face and shoulders.

In some strange way, she thought dazedly, her skin warming, it was one of the most intimate things he had ever done to her. Almost more so than sex itself.

Then he lifted the scented auburn mass in both hands and she felt his lips caress the exposed and vulnerable nape of her neck.

Her entire body shivered at the brush of his mouth and she wondered if he knew this, and realised it was all too likely. That he knew everything about female bodies, their responses and reactions. Knew—and exploited his knowledge. So any sign of weakness on her part could be her ultimate downfall, and she must never forget that. Never.

It also seemed, from the smoothness of his skin against hers, that he'd had the promised shave—presumably while she'd been preparing dinner.

Advance planning, she thought, digging her nails into the palms of her hands. He said softly into her ear, 'Don't make me wait too long, *cara*,' and moved away, but only, she realised at

once, to undress. She knew, too, that he expected her to do the
same, there in front of him. And that there was no real reason to
hesitate, because he'd already seen her naked. Had already
touched and kissed every inch of her, his astonishing patience
pitched against her stubborn will.

She had nothing left to hide from him, but her hands were still
slow and reluctant as she tugged her sweater over her head and
tossed it on to the nearby chair. She unzipped her cords and
eased them down over her hips, stepping out of them in order to
do the same with her tights, all the time keeping her back resolutely turned to him.

His approach was soundless. She only realised he was
standing close behind her when she reached round awkwardly
to unhook her bra and felt him move her hands aside so that he
could perform the task himself.

He slid the straps from her shoulders, kissing the faint marks
they'd left on her skin, then removed the little garment completely, dropping it to the floor.

He drew her slowly back against him, her head resting against
his bare chest, letting her feel the heat of his aroused body. His
lips feathered kisses down the side of her throat as his hands
cupped her small firm breasts, his fingertips drawing lingering
circles round her nipples, making them rise proudly like dusky
roses in bud.

'*Bellissima.*' His voice was husky. '*Deliciosa.*'

He let one hand move slowly downwards with smooth and deliberate purpose, his fingers slipping under the edge of her lacy
briefs to seek the silken triangle at the joining of her thighs.

'No.' Her voice was a gasp as her hand fastened round his wrist,
halting him, forbidding him to go any further. 'Stop—please.'

He paused, his fingers splayed across the flat plane of her belly.

He said quietly, 'Tell me something, Emilia *mia*. Why are you
so afraid of pleasure?'

'It has nothing to do with fear,' Emily said stonily, aware that she
was shaking inside. She pulled away from him, drawing a deep
breath. Staring in front of her. Not at him. Not daring to look at him.

'You take three years from my life, you destroy my hopes of

future happiness, and then you take me.' Her voice rose. 'And I'm supposed to be grateful—and willing?'

She shook her head. 'In your dreams, *signore*. Besides, being mauled by you is far from my idea of pleasure,' she added defiantly.

For a long moment Raf did not move or speak. Then suddenly he was no longer holding her—touching her, and she was aware of him moving away across the room. Of the slight creak of the mattress as he got into bed.

For a few heartbeats she paused uncertainly, then fumbled off her briefs, putting them with the rest of her clothing.

Drawing a deep, jagged breath, she turned and walked to the bed, resisting the impulse to cover herself with her hands. But far from gloating avidly over her approach, Raf was lying on his back, staring up at the ceiling.

Emily slid hurriedly under the covers, pulling them up over her shoulders, then lay still, waiting for him to reach for her.

But he did not move and, as the long minutes passed, her tension grew and the deeper inner trembling intensified.

At last he turned his head and looked at her, the hazel eyes cool and steady.

'I will make a bargain with you, Emilia,' he said. 'Kiss me and I will ask nothing else from you tonight.'

Emily stared at him, then found a voice from somewhere, almost squeaky with surprise. 'You'll let me—just go to sleep—for a kiss?

'I have just said so.'

'But I thought you wanted…' *She didn't just think—she knew. When he'd been holding her just now the evidence of his desire for her had been frank and unequivocal.*

'Undoubtedly I did.' His mouth twisted. 'But I find I am no longer in the mood to treat you as gently as I should, given your inexperience.' He added coldly, 'So perhaps I deserve a little of your gratitude, after all, if my only demand is a kiss. You are escaping lightly, believe me.'

He paused. 'Do you accept my offer, Contessa?'

'I—I suppose so.'

'*Bene.*' He waited for a moment, watching her, brows raised.

'But you will need to come closer, *cara mia*,' he added, his tone almost bored. 'Sadly, it is impossible for you to reach me from such a distance.'

Biting her lip, Emily edged warily across the bed. When she was within range, she leaned over him, her lips brushing swiftly and awkwardly against his in the most fleeting of contact.

There was a tingling silence, then he said softly, 'That may be your idea of a kiss, Emilia, but it is not mine. There is ice enough outside the house at this time. I do not require it here in my bed.'

She stiffened, needled by the faint derision in his voice. 'I'm sorry if you're not satisfied…'

'Now that, as we both know, is a lie,' he said. 'But now is not the time to discuss my level of satisfaction, or lack of it, and what you might do to improve it.' He allowed her a moment to assimilate that, then added, 'At the moment, you are simply required to—try a little harder.'

He raised a hand, cupping the back of her head, his fingers tangling in her hair, so that she could not pull away. 'So, kiss me again, *cara mia*,' he invited quietly. 'Kiss me as you did on that long ago night in your father's house.'

'But—but that was when I thought you were—someone else.' Her voice was a breath.

'Did you truly, *bella mia*?' Raf asked cynically. 'I have often wondered how that could be possible. But, if it is easier for you, pretend once more that I am someone else. I promise I will not even ask his name.'

His hand was impelling her down to him, bringing her ever nearer to his waiting mouth.

And this time, as her lips touched the firm warmth of his, she found herself allowing the contact to lengthen—even to linger. Because, she told herself in growing confusion, this was what he wanted. And it was such a minor demand for him to make after—after all those others.

Suddenly he moved, reversing their positions smoothly and swiftly, so that she was lying on the pillow, looking up at him, her startled eyes widening.

And then he was kissing her, his mouth moving on hers slowly and achingly at first, then with a hard, deepening urgency—a hunger that made the soft, trembling contours of her lips feel bruised.

Until she could scarcely breathe. Or think rationally any more.

Or why else would she have found that, against all expectation, she wanted to return the sensuous pressure that he was subjecting her to? That she needed to learn the lines of his mouth as thoroughly as he was exploring hers? And, maybe, even more…

And then, with almost shocking suddenness, it was over, and he was lifting himself away from her.

'A great improvement,' he said in a tone so impersonal that Emily, still dazed, almost expected him to give her marks out of ten. He ran a careless finger down the curve of her cheek. 'Now, sleep well, *cara*,' he added lightly. 'And may all your dreams be sweet.'

He turned to switch off the lamp, leaving her with an unwanted, but potent image of the long, supple line of his naked back before the room was plunged into darkness.

Emily turned away too, almost scuttling to the opposite side of the bed, lying, taut and breathless, on its furthermost edge as she waited for her heartbeat to regain its normality.

She was shaken to the core by her own reaction. Bitterly ashamed of her own weakness. And surprised too that Raf had actually kept his word, had not taken further advantage of her.

Yet Emily knew she had by no means escaped unscathed. That there was an even more worrying aspect of the situation that she somehow had to confront.

That long ago night…

Those were the words that were now coming back to haunt her. His unfounded but still disturbing suggestion that she might have gone into his arms knowing full well that he was not Simon.

Indicating that her female instinct should have stopped her before she'd got within a yard of him, let alone thrown herself at him.

But that's nonsense, she told herself. It was dark, and I was very young and very stressed—nervous as hell—not thinking straight. Besides, it was Simon I was expecting. No one else. Because Raf was with Jilly. I—I knew that. Knew that, if she had her way, there was no reason to expect him back before breakfast.

And, anyway, as soon as I realised my mistake, I pushed him away instantly—immediately, she thought defensively. Of course

I did. Although I admit that it should not have got to that stage. That obviously I should have known as soon as he first touched me. And that it should never—ever—have gone as far as it did.

But it was an honest error. And Raf has no right and no reason to imply anything different. As if I'd *wanted* to find out what being in his arms—being kissed by him—might feel like.

Which, she told herself hotly, is a shameful inference to draw from an—an innocent blunder.

Yet suddenly Emily found she was shivering, wrapping her arms round her body in an involuntary gesture of self-protection.

Because she was bitterly aware that she'd never been able to forget that brief moment in time, no matter how hard she'd tried. That she'd seen it as a warning not to allow him anywhere near her again.

But was that because she could not trust him, as Raf himself had proved only last night, justifying all her worst fears? Or was it—could it be—because she was afraid she might not be able to trust herself?

Could it be possible that there'd been one second—one infinitesimal moment on that long ago night when she hadn't wanted to step back? When, incredibly, she'd wanted to press herself closer to the hardening danger of his body and offer her parted lips for his deeper exploration?

She hadn't been unfaithful to Simon—of course not. But instinct had told her she'd approached some danger zone that she hadn't known existed till then. So she'd buried all the doubts—the unanswered questions far, far down in her psyche.

But now Raf's mocking challenge had brought them all raging back to the surface to torment her, testing the validity of her claim of 'an honest error'.

Yes, it was still a terrible mistake to have made, but whether it was 'honest' or 'innocent' was now wide open to question.

Because she'd never managed to completely erase the memory of that barely discernible flicker of physical excitement.

And, if she was being truly honest, it wasn't the only time that she'd reacted in that particular way.

My wedding night in Italy, she thought, swallowing. When I saw him walk into the bedroom and felt myself start to tremble inside. Yes, I was scared, at first anyway, but that wasn't all of it, and I—I knew it.

Because I suddenly found myself remembering that other night and his arms holding me—the touch—the taste of his mouth. And wondered...

And, for a moment, I almost forgot that he'd married me solely out of a sense of obligation to my father. Although Rafaele soon reminded me, of course. Spelled out chapter and verse, then walked away.

While I told myself I should be relieved that he didn't want me and even more thankful that I hadn't made a fool of myself by smiling at him, or giving any other indication that he might be welcome to stay.

And yet there'd been times during that first year of marriage when Raf's constant visits had been difficult to bear. Dreams, too, that she'd burned to remember.

But, eventually, as he'd begun to stay away and the rumours that he'd resumed his bachelor lifestyle had begun to circulate, Emily had been able to convince herself that it had all been a temporary aberration on her part, with no connection to the future she was planning for herself.

And when Simon came back and told me he'd never stopped loving me, she thought, I felt justified somehow. I was glad I could tell him that there'd never been—anyone else for me, and that we could start again—together. That I'd belong to him—and him alone.

Fine words, yet, so far, I haven't shed a single tear for him. Is it possible that I always suspected, deep down, that I was just a means to an end? My father's credulous heiress, looking for love in increasingly hopeless places?

Because I haven't been very lucky in either of my suitors. One of them sold me out and the other used me to repay an old debt.

Which doesn't leave me with many illusions about myself and maybe I will be able to cry about that one day. Before I begin to sort out exactly who I am and what I really want. But not yet.

Because I have to get through this somehow and I can't afford tears or self-pity. I need to survive.

She closed her eyes resolutely, then opened them again.

That long ago night...

It occurred to her suddenly that this was the first time Raf had ever mentioned it. Up to now, he'd always behaved as if it had never happened. But then, she thought, he'd never required her to kiss him before either.

Not that it meant anything, she added hastily. It was just another way of asserting his male dominance. Another ploy to humiliate her, as she'd embarrassed him over the annulment issue.

But she would never let him see that it mattered. Not that— or anything else he might do to her. She would shore up the control she'd so painfully acquired. And there would be no more moments of weakness or inappropriate curiosity about how it might be if she ever surrendered herself completely to his love-making, she told herself fiercely.

Because, one day soon, he would become tired of this fruitless battle of wills and decide to let her go and she wanted to be able to walk away, her head held high.

And now, she thought, swallowing past the tightness in her throat, I have to stop thinking about him and try to sleep.

She dozed eventually, but it was no peaceful rest. She was assailed by snatches of dreams peopled by shadowed figures with faces she did not recognise, who turned away as she struggled to reach them across bleak and barren landscapes.

In the end she was never sure what woke her. But as she opened her eyes to the pale grey light filtering through the curtains, she had a overwhelming impression of being warm, relaxed and deliciously comfortable. All this, she thought drowsily, in total contrast to her miserable night with its fragmented dreams.

Yet, as her awareness increased, several disturbing facts made themselves evident. For one, she was no longer lying on the far side of the bed, clinging to its edge as if stranded on the north face of the Eiger.

Somehow, in the night, she had moved back across the broad expanse of the mattress to where Raf was lying.

But she wasn't just next to him, for heaven's sake, but right up against him as if she'd been glued to his spine. Her legs had somehow become entangled with his and her body had adapted every inch of itself to fit the long, lean curve of his back, her breasts crushed against its hard muscularity, and her arm draped round his waist. Moreover, her face was pressed between his shoulder blades, so that her nose and mouth were filled with the warm, clean scent of his skin.

Emily lay for a moment, hardly daring to breathe, intensely conscious of the violent, erratic beat of her heart. Out of one nightmare into another, she thought with horror. Dear God, I'm practically *inside* him.

But how could it possibly have happened? It had to be her own doing, because Raf clearly hadn't moved an inch and, fortunately, was still sleeping deeply and peacefully.

Slowly, her bottom lip caught in her teeth, she began to detach herself from him, little by little, before edging stealthily backwards, every nerve-ending attuned to the possibility that he might wake up, and then…

But she wouldn't consider that. She'd just concentrate on freeing herself. All the same, it seemed an eternity before she could slide out from under the covers altogether and she stifled a gasp as her warm skin encountered the icy air in the room.

Tiptoeing about, trying to avoid any sound, she found her nightdress and pulled it on. It might not be picturesque, and it certainly wasn't sexy, but it provided a much-needed layer of insulation, she thought, topping it with a quilted gilet for good measure.

Noiselessly, she drew back the curtains and looked out. It had snowed again in the night, she saw without pleasure, and there were still a few flakes whirling past the window from the slate-grey sky.

And small wonder that it was freezing, she thought, testing the radiator with a cautious finger. The heating wasn't on, which meant there was probably something wrong with the boiler.

She groaned silently. This was all she needed.

She went softly out of the room and down the stairs to the kitchen. Coffee was the priority, she told herself as she filled the kettle and set it to boil. Strong and very hot.

She wandered into the living room, opening the curtains, shaking up the sofa cushions and collecting the glasses from the previous evening.

The kettle should have been boiling by the time she returned to the kitchen, but there was no cheerful sound of seething water or any trace of steam from the spout and it was stone-cold to her cautious touch.

She suddenly remembered Angus's casual warning about power failures and the way the lights had flickered the night before and said aloud, 'Oh, *no*...'

She tried the light switch by the door, again with no result, then returned to the sink and turned on the hot tap, willing there to be at least some hot water left in the tank, but it was like putting her hand into the ice of a mountain stream and she bowed her head defeatedly.

'You are feeling the cold, *carissima*?'

The softly spoken words made her turn quickly to see Raf lounging in the archway, his dark face alight with amusement as he studied how she was dressed.

'Isn't it obvious?' she snapped defensively, observing that, by contrast and in spite of the temperature, he was wearing nothing but a towel knotted loosely round his hips.

His grin widened. He strolled across, sliding both arms round her waist, his lips nuzzling her neck. 'Then you should have stayed in bed with me,' he whispered. 'I find I am in a much better mood this morning.'

'Then I hope it continues,' Emily said bitterly, trying to free herself from his clasp. 'Especially when I tell you we have no electricity.'

'*Davvero*?' He sounded more interested than perturbed. 'Well, it is not the end of the world.'

'No?' She wrenched herself away and stepped backwards. 'You enjoy being without heat or light, do you? I don't think so.'

'We have a fire, candles and a stove to cook on.' He shrugged. 'Life goes on.'

'But there's no hot water. I can't even have a bloody bath.' She raised two clenched fists. 'Oh, God, why did I ever come to this hellish place?'

'I think, Emilia *mia*,' he drawled, 'that is a question you should answer for yourself rather than troubling *Il Signore*.' He paused. 'Your father told me once he feared he had over-indulged you. I have often thought since that he was right.'

'Don't you dare mention my father,' she flared. 'What do you imagine he'd think of you, if he knew you'd broken your word about this marriage?'

'He asked me to give you time,' he said. 'He did not expect me to wait for ever. So he would assume we had reached some accommodation with each other at last and already have begun to look forward to his grandchildren.' His tone was brusque. 'Now, let us leave your flights of fancy and be practical.' He opened a cupboard and extracted several large saucepans, along with a huge preserving pan.

'If you wish to bathe, you may do so. It will not be luxurious, *naturalmente*, but it is the best that can be managed.'

Emily's nose wrinkled doubtfully. 'You mean we're going to carry hot water—all the way upstairs—in pans?'

'No,' he said wearily. 'I am going to do it for you, so you will not be inconvenienced in any way, Contessa.' He took out a much smaller pan. 'And before you ask, this is to boil water for coffee. I think I may need it.'

She bit her lip. 'That's why I came downstairs to—to make coffee…'

'I think not.' His smile was swift and ironic. 'You came down, *cara mia*, because you realised you had spent the night nestling against me in a way it took all my self-control to resist and you found the discovery an embarrassment.'

He walked past her to the sink and began to fill the preserving pan with water.

'I suggest you wait upstairs,' he added over his shoulder. 'And be sure to put some cold water in the bath first. I would not wish you to be scalded.'

She was scalded already, Emily thought furiously, as she marched out of the kitchen. Burning from head to foot. And not just because he clearly believed she was running scared after last night's gaffe. The claim that she was some kind of spoiled brat rankled even more, implying that he and her father had calmly discussed her faults and failings before the marriage.

I'm surprised he didn't ask to see my school reports or examine my teeth, she fumed under her breath as she climbed the stairs, trying not to trip on the trailing nightgown.

And if he has some idea that finding my arm round him in the night meant anything, he can think again—and fast.

But she took his advice about the cold water before retiring to the bedroom and assembling her clothing for the day. As many layers as possible, she thought. Warm tights under her cords and a long-sleeved T-shirt under her thickest sweater. And dismissed the sly inner voice which suggested that she could be wrapping herself against more than the weather.

She had just finished making the bed when Raf appeared in the doorway.

'Your bath awaits, *signora*.' He paused. 'It reminds me that I must instruct Gaspare to engage a personal maid for you. A girl with muscles.'

'That,' said Emily coldly, 'is entirely unnecessary.'

'I disagree.' He gave her nightgown another long look. 'She will also conduct a complete review of your wardrobe and list what is required.' He added softly, 'I shall choose your lingerie myself—and it will not be black.'

He doesn't forget a thing, Emily thought bitterly. She lifted her chin. 'Thank you, but my existing clothes are perfectly adequate for my life.'

'But not for the life you will lead with me,' he told her with finality.

'And where am I expected to shop for this new wardrobe?' she challenged. 'At Valentina X, maybe?'

There was the faintest of pauses, then Raf said softly, 'Of course, if that is what you wish. Although I think Signora Colona may cater, perhaps, for more sophisticated tastes.'

He allowed her to assimilate that, then smiled at her. 'But the choice is entirely yours, *cara*. Every designer in Italy will welcome the Contessa Di Salis.'

'How very exciting for me,' she said. 'Now, excuse me please, or my bath will be getting cold.'

But of course it wasn't. In fact the temperature was perfect and, annoyingly, he had even added some of her favourite bath oil.

Swiftly, she shed her nightgown and stepped in, reaching for the soap and rubbing it fiercely into her skin in a vain attempt to conceal the fact that she was smarting already.

Confronting Raf about his mistress had achieved nothing, she thought. He'd remained completely unfazed. Whereas she'd probably sounded young and silly. But not jealous, she prayed, closing her eyes. Oh, please, not jealous. Because it wasn't true—it wasn't true at all...

The creak of a board brought her abruptly back to the here and now and the realisation that Raf had walked into the bathroom, carrying another large pan.

'It's all right, thank you,' she said, trying to fold herself into startled invisibility. If she lived to be a hundred, she thought, she would never become accustomed to his casual attitude to nudity—hers or his. 'The water's fine as it is.'

'But not for me, *carissima*,' he said silkily. 'I like the temperature raised a little.' He poured the contents of the pan carefully into the bath, dropped the towel he was wearing and joined her.

'What do you think you're doing?' She hated the breathless note in her voice as she tried to retreat into some distant corner of the bath that didn't actually exist.

'Washing,' he said and held out a hand. 'The soap, *sposa mia*, if you please.'

Numbly, she handed it to him, finding a voice from somewhere. 'It doesn't matter to you that I might prefer some privacy?'

'And you may have it, once I no longer have to act as water carrier.' He was briskly lathering his shoulders and chest. 'But, until the power returns, we share.' He scooped up handfuls of water, spilling the shining droplets over his head.

'Thank you,' she said. 'But I've finished.'

It was awkward leaving the bath under his sardonic gaze, but she managed it, winding the waiting towel round her like a sarong, covering herself against him.

'Would you care to wash my back before you go?' he asked.

Emily bit her lip. 'No,' she said, stonily. 'I wouldn't.'

His mouth twisted. 'You did not find touching me so distasteful last night, *mia bella*.'

'Because,' she said, 'I was still pretending you were someone else, *signore*.' She added coolly, 'I find it works very well.'

And she walked out of the bathroom, the edge of the towel following her like a train.

CHAPTER EIGHT

EMILY sat curled up despondently in the corner of the sofa. The chicken bones were simmering on the kitchen stove with some attendant vegetables, but whether they'd ever become edible soup was anyone's guess.

What was more, she'd arrived downstairs to discover that Raf, in between his water heating activities, had taken the time to clean the grate and light the fire in the living room, so conditions weren't as arctic as she'd anticipated.

Which made her parting shot to him in the bathroom seem even more ungracious.

On the other hand, she didn't want to feel grateful to him. She wanted to keep her resentment alive. Needed to hate what he'd done to her, as well as what he had planned for her immediate future.

Last night, she'd slept, melded with him. Had become totally imbued with him. But how and why it had happened was beyond her. She supposed it must have been her subconscious reaction to that lingering kiss that had drawn her to him, and that, in itself, was deeply disturbing.

Except that it was over now, she reminded himself swiftly. This was another day altogether and she had to stay strong and not let herself remember the silken texture of his skin under her cheek—her mouth.

Or how her arm had encircled his lean waist. The way her body had seemed to fit with his, as if it had been designed for that purpose alone.

Above all, she had to blind herself to the sheer male physicality of him. In spite of herself, she could not ignore how sensational he looked without his clothes, and how the grace and strength of his nakedness turned her mouth dry and transformed her own body to an aching, melting heat that made her feel ashamed. And scared.

Which had made it so necessary to toss him that scornful comment and walk away just now.

Because she couldn't let herself touch him, she thought. Not again. She couldn't risk it, any more than she dared to allow him to touch her. The opportunities for self-betrayal were far too dangerous.

She sighed. She was certainly succeeding in turning this into the honeymoon from hell, yet, at the same time, it wasn't the unalloyed triumph she'd expected.

She heard him coming downstairs and tensed, expecting some kind of repercussion, but Raf was zipping himself into his parka as he reached the bottom of the stairs and barely glanced at her. For one panicky moment she thought he might be cutting his losses and leaving, abandoning her here to her own devices, then realised he didn't have his bag with him.

'You—you're going out?' she ventured.

'As you see. I shall walk down to the village and see what food is to be had,' he said. 'We cannot exist on a few chicken bones.'

'Is it safe to do that—with all this snow?'

'Yes,' he said. 'Or I would not try.'

Emily stood up. 'Then I'll come with you.'

'You have developed a sudden taste for my company?' His mouth curled. 'Impossible.' He paused. 'Or are you hoping to encounter your admirer, perhaps?'

'Please don't be absurd,' she said. 'It's simply that I'm getting cabin fever cooped up like this.'

He looked at her sceptically. 'It will be treacherous underfoot,' he warned.

As if the conditions indoors were so ideal, she thought.

'It is a pity I did not bring my skis with me,' he went on. 'Ah, but you do not ski, I believe, *cara*.'

Just in time she remembered she'd told him that when he'd

invited her to spend his New Year holiday with him in the Dolomites the first year of their marriage.

'A pity you did not tell your father so,' he added silkily. 'He spent a great deal on your school trips to Switzerland each winter, I understand, and all for nothing. It would have saddened him.'

He paused, watching the swift annoyed colour rise in her face.

'However, there are some rubber boots in the cellar,' he continued. 'They may be too large, and the tops appear to have been chewed by rats, but they might be of assistance.'

She shuddered. 'My own boots will be fine. I'll manage.'

Only she didn't. One minute she found herself skidding on a frozen patch, the next she was above her knees in soft snow, and forced to grab at Raf's arm to stop herself from falling.

As soon as she'd recovered her balance, she apologised, her face flushing even more deeply.

'This is a bad idea.' He sounded faintly bored. 'I will take you back, *cara*, before you break something.'

As she reluctantly accepted his assistance to turn awkwardly and make her sliding way back to the cottage, she could only wish it would be his neck.

But, standing by the window, watching him disappear down the track and out of sight, she found herself feeling oddly forlorn and regretting that she hadn't tried the rat-nibbled wellies after all.

He seemed to be gone for ever and she was on edge the whole time, imagining that her ill-wishing had somehow taken effect and he was lying in a drift with compound fractures and acute hypothermia.

'And then what would I do?' she demanded aloud, defending any concern she might have purely on the grounds of self-interest.

She began wandering almost compulsively from room to room, inventing tasks for herself, like dragging the heavy fur rug that lay in front of the fire to the door and shaking it so vigorously that she almost fell over again.

However, her chicken bone concoction seemed to be smelling more appetising by the moment, which was mildly encouraging.

She was prodding it doubtfully with a fork, when she finally heard the door open and flew into the living room to find Raf heaving two carrier bags on to the table.

But she swallowed back her instinctive Thank God, replacing it with a tart, 'You took your time.'

His brows lifted in hauteur. 'Perhaps you wish to go in my place on the next occasion? You are welcome to do so, although I doubt you will do any better. The good Signora provides a limited choice.' He counted on his fingers. 'No garlic, no fresh herbs, no olive oil worthy of the name and no pasta except something in a can.

'It is little wonder that Marcello and Fiona bring supplies with them and eat out as often as possible,' he added grimly. 'But for the weather, we would have done the same.'

How could he talk like that, she wondered with a pang, as if they were a normal couple, enjoying a break together? She lifted her chin. 'But for the weather, I would be long gone, *signore*.'

His voice was soft. 'If it comforts you to think so, *signora*.'

He began to unpack the bags, producing vegetables, apples, bread rolls, milk and some pallid-looking sausages, along with tins of tomatoes and haricot beans plus a couple of packs of meat.

'They're frozen,' she discovered. 'How can that be?'

'The shop operates an emergency generator.' He took out a packet of very pink ham, fashioned into squares, and looked at it with a faint sigh.

'However, the Signora tells me the power will be restored by the end of the day and also that a thaw is expected later in the week.' The firm mouth curled. 'I refer only to the weather, you understand.'

She said with difficulty, 'Raf, don't—please. I—I can't help the way I am.'

'I do not agree. I think you have no idea how you could be, *mia cara*.' His tone was hard. 'Nor will you permit yourself to find out. But that is your choice.'

He walked towards the door. 'Now I am going to dig paths to the log store and the place where the coal is kept in case you need them.'

She tried to say, 'Thank you,' but the words wouldn't come, so she nodded and turned away.

Alone again, she began to put the groceries away, aware that her hands were shaking and that her eyes kept blurring.

But what was there to cry about, she wondered, when, as he'd said, she'd made her choice? And when all she had to do was stick to it.

Because, for him, it was just a game, like chess. He made a move, she blocked it somehow. And even this would pass, she whispered to herself, if she simply—stood firm and waited for him to tire of this perpetual stalemate.

As he surely would, she thought, and tasted the acrid tears in her throat.

It was not the easiest day she had ever spent. Raf busied himself outside, and she made sure she followed his example indoors. Because that was the best way to stop herself from thinking.

She strained the chicken stock, adding potatoes and leeks as well as the remaining meat to the mixture, then let it cook slowly, producing a soup that was thick and surprisingly flavoursome, and heating some of the rolls to go with it.

'That was excellent,' Raf said as he finished his second bowl. 'Working in the air makes you hungry.'

'Have you finished all your digging?'

'Not yet. I decided also to clear a path down to the road.'

'You'll be exhausted.' She spoke without thinking and felt the colour storm her face when he laughed, getting to his feet.

'I am sure you hope so, *carissima*, but you will be disappointed.'

He paused, then added lightly, 'At least in that regard.'

Which was an unequivocal declaration of intent, Emily thought, staring after him, her heart beating uncomfortably, as he disappeared outside again. Sending out a clear signal that tonight he would not be satisfied with just a kiss.

In an effort at distraction, she found an elderly pack of cards and spent an hour or so playing solitaire, but without success, finding herself invariably thwarted at the last minute. How very like real life, she thought crossly, pushing the cards together.

She went into the kitchen and began assembling the evening meal. The meat was still frozen, so she decided to use the unpromising sausages instead. Cooking them in batter would disguise their major faults, she thought, measuring flour into a bowl, and an onion gravy would also be a plus.

By the time Raf came in, she'd made up the living room fire and lit the candles. He was sitting on the sofa, pulling off his boots, when she emerged from the kitchen and his brows lifted as he realised she was bringing him a mug of freshly made coffee.

'You are the perfect wife, *carissima*,' he told her lightly and she turned away, biting her lip. Except in one respect, she thought, but no doubt he considered that was merely a matter of time.

While their meal was cooking, she sat opposite him and pretended to read in the intimacy of the flickering light, while he was absorbed in another chess problem, and occasionally stole a glance at him when she felt it was safe to do so.

He'd have fitted well into an earlier century, she thought, wearing silk and velvet, although she was only just becoming used to him in jeans and sweaters rather than the customary elegance of formal designer suits. She could imagine him standing in the shadows of some Renaissance court, his hand on the jewelled hilt of a sword, or riding into a conquered city at the head of his men, his eyes scanning the captive women lined up for his inspection, and his choice.

She caught herself there and halted, because that was rather too apposite, she thought wryly. Yet, at the same time, she found herself wanting to laugh at her own nonsense.

'What are you thinking?' The quiet question startled her.

'Why do you ask?' she parried.

'Because you are smiling at your thoughts, *cara*, and that is something of a novelty in my acquaintance with you.'

So, she thought, he'd been watching her too, which was distinctly unnerving.

She shrugged lightly. 'But you can't just ask,' she said. 'You have to say—penny for your thoughts. And pay up,' she added, playing for time.

Raf reached into a pocket and tossed a coin to her. 'So—tell me.'

'Ten pence,' she marvelled. 'I'm not sure it's worth such a vast sum. I was just wondering how people managed in the past when candles were all the light they had.'

'With their eyesight in ruins, perhaps,' Raf said drily. 'But they would have used many more, I think. Great, glittering chandeli-

ers and banks of candelabra. It would have been—amazing—
spettacoloso.'

'Also a hell of a fire risk.'

'That too,' he agreed. 'But, I wonder again, *bella mia*, what
you were truly thinking.'

She put her book aside, her smile swift and taut as she rose.
'Right now, I think I should check on supper.'

Which had turned out far better than she could have hoped,
the sausages looking brown and succulent, their surrounding
batter golden and well-risen.

'Toad-in-the-hole,' she announced as she placed the dish in
front of him.

'*Santa Madonna*,' he said with disbelief. 'Tell me the name
again.'

She complied. 'Also bubble and squeak,' she added
demurely, indicating the bowl of potatoes fried with cabbage
and chopped onion.

His eyes were alive with laughter as they met hers across the
glow of the candles. 'I think you are winding me up, *carissima*.'

'Not at all.' She paused. 'Although it isn't the gourmet food
you're accustomed to, *signore*.'

He took a substantial helping. 'I have no complaints, believe
me, *signora*.'

It was the most companionable time they'd spent together. For
the most part, they talked about food—their likes and dislikes—
and some of the best and worst meals they'd ever eaten, although
Raf won hands down here with a pungent description of some of
the more exotic courses he'd been served in the Far East, making
Emily shudder and gurgle with laughter at the same time.

'You understand now why I might find toad-in-the-hole disturbing.' He refilled her wineglass.

'It's only fresh fruit for dessert, I'm afraid.' She began to
collect the used dishes together. 'And not much choice at that.
You can have an apple or an apple.'

He pretended to consider. 'I think I would prefer an apple.'

As he followed her into the kitchen with the dirty plates,
Emily, putting cutlery in the sink, glanced through the window
and gave a squeak.

'I can see a light.' She pointed. 'Several lights—down there in the distance. Glory hallelujah, I think the power's back on. Try the switch.'

'I must do this?' He sounded rueful. 'Candlelight is gentler, *bella mia*. It has more—atmosphere.'

But not the sort she necessarily wished to encourage, Emily realised, her throat tightening.

'On the other hand,' she said, 'I don't want to end up with ruined eyesight.'

'No.' His hand moved to the switch and the kitchen surged into a sudden brightness that broke any spell there might briefly have been. 'I shall go to check on the boiler—ensure that tonight the radiators are *hot* in the morning.'

'And the water,' she reminded him. 'You won't want any more treks upstairs with heavy pans.'

'Ah,' Raf said softly. 'But even that had its compensations.' He took an apple from the bowl on the counter top and disappeared off to the cellar, leaving Emily's sense of apprehension growing by the minute.

It was one thing to repeat to herself that she'd already experienced the worst he could do to her. However, believing it was something else again.

And she was nervous about filling the hours until bedtime. Scared that she might find herself watching him again in the lamplit silence and that he might interpret the confusion of her thoughts in his own way.

Because she wasn't sure she was the same person as the outraged defiant girl of two nights ago, who'd fought not just his possession of her but the treachery of her own senses, and achieved a kind of victory.

Since their marriage, she thought, she'd taught herself quite deliberately to regard Raf as a stranger—an occasional guest to be accorded a polite welcome on arrival, then more or less ignored until his departure.

During the first year, of course, she'd been showered by joint invitations from local people, eager to offer hospitality to the newlyweds. 'We do so hope we'll meet your charming husband this time,' had been the general theme. But she'd refused them all, mendaciously citing Raf's hectic work schedule as an excuse.

'We are not a couple,' she'd wanted to say so many times. 'We are two separate people trapped in a situation.'

And, as his visits had diminished, it had become easier to think about him less. Even to pretend that he did not really exist as a man. That he was just a disembodied voice on a phone, or a name on a letter.

But now, in the space of forty-eight short hours, he'd placed himself centre-stage in her awareness in every possible way. And it wasn't just a sexual thing either. In some strange way she was beginning to accept his presence—becoming used to having him around. There'd even been moments over supper when, however reluctantly, she'd actually found herself enjoying his company.

If only I wasn't married to him—or if the marriage had stayed in name only—maybe we might have been friends, she thought with an odd wistfulness. Then remembered that he'd once offered friendship, which she'd rejected too. What she could not seem to recall was—the reason for her refusal.

But that's in the past, she told herself decisively. It was tonight she needed to be concerned about, now that Raf had made it clear he intended to take full advantage of his sexual prerogative.

She needed to devise some way of holding him off, and quickly too. Yet, somehow, she didn't think that simply inventing a headache would work, while pretending she had her period would simply cause complications later.

Maybe some version of the truth would serve her better, she thought unhappily. An attempt to convince him, somehow, that he was wasting his time with her and that he should give up whatever game he was playing and go back to his mistress.

But would he see it that way?

'Why are you staring into space, *cara*?'

His voice behind her made her start violently.

She turned, flushing. 'I was just thinking I'd leave the washing-up until morning,' she said evasively. 'I—I'm feeling horribly tired.'

'*Davvero?*' Raf's expression was sardonic as he disposed of his apple core in the kitchen bin and rinsed his fingers under the tap. 'Then, as soon as we have had coffee, we will go to bed, *mia bella*.'

Emily bit her lip. 'That—isn't what I meant.'

'No,' he said. 'That, at least, is the truth.' He paused. 'It is time we talked a little, Emilia. Wait for me by the fire.'

It was a command, not a request, and there was a note in his voice that warned her not to risk defiance.

She trailed unwillingly into the living room and sat down on the edge of the sofa, her hands clamped together in her lap, as she wondered what he planned to say. Perhaps he'd come to the same conclusion as herself and had decided to draw a final line under this ill-judged marriage.

But, when he arrived with the coffee, he didn't take his usual seat on the sofa opposite, but came instead to sit beside her. Making Emily realise, dry-mouthed, that she'd hoped for altogether too much.

'No coffee for me, thanks,' she declined curtly as he picked up the cafetiére.

'You are afraid it will keep you awake?' He sounded faintly amused as he filled his own cup.

She sent him a fulminating look, resenting the way he was lounging there, so much at his ease, as he drank his coffee, his jeans-clad thigh only an inch or two from hers, then turned her attention to the fire, staring at the small blue flames licking round the logs until her eyes blurred.

Eventually, she heard him replace his cup on the tray and tensed.

There was a long pause, then he said quietly, 'Emilia—please look at me, *cara mia*. I cannot talk to your back.'

'Is there any need for us to talk at all?' She turned her head unwillingly, absorbing the taut, unsmiling lines of his face.

'I think so.' He hesitated. '*Carissima*, I would be the first to admit that our marriage has begun badly, and for that I blame myself.'

'That's big of you,' she said.

'Our life together was wrong from those first nights and days three years ago.' His hands closed on hers, unclasping them and stroking her rigid fingers.

'Yet that could change—so very easily,' he went on. 'Please believe that.'

'I do,' she said stonily. 'But only if you were to leave—give me the divorce we agreed at the beginning.'

'You may feel that,' he said. 'But I say there is an alternative. That perhaps we might find a little happiness together.'

His fingertips caressed the curve of her face, tracing tiny patterns on the line of her throat.

He said very softly, 'You don't think, my beautiful wife, that if I tried—if I really tried—I might coax you to be—more compliant?'

He was half smiling as he spoke, but the hazel eyes as they met hers were rueful—almost tender.

Her breath caught as it occurred to her in that moment, with all the stunning force of a blow, that with very little effort Count Rafaele Di Salis could probably coax the heart out of her body.

She thought desperately, Dear God, what's happening to me—and how can I stop it—now—before it's too late?'

His arm encircled her shoulders, drawing her closer. 'Don't fight me any longer, Emilia.' His voice was a breath against her ear. 'Tonight, let us take each other as lovers. Allow me to show you, *carissima*, what joy can be.'

She said, quietly and clearly, 'You recently implied, *signore*, that I was spoiled. I think you've been over-indulged too—by a succession of women who've allowed you to think you're irresistible. And, to them, perhaps you are. But not to me.'

She paused. 'And I have absolutely no plans to sacrifice my self-respect in order to provide you with an hour's amusement in bed.'

There was a silence. She felt him tense—the arm round her shoulders become a bar of steel. He said harshly, 'An hour, you say? I think not. After all, we shall not be making love, so a few minutes only will suffice. And we do not need a bed.'

Before she could move or protest, he was lifting her off the sofa and down on to the thick hearthrug, kneeling over her as he unfastened her cord trousers, dragging them down from her hips together with her underwear, then wrenching at his own zip.

Gasping, Emily tried to struggle—to push him away. 'What are you doing?'

He controlled her effortlessly, nudging her thighs apart with a knee. 'How does it seem?' he countered harshly. 'You are not open to any form of persuasion, *signora*. You prefer to close your heart and mind against me, so this is what you must expect.'

'Oh, God, you don't mean this...' Her voice broke as she felt the hardness of him seeking her moist and yielding heat, then entering her with one strong, implacable thrust.

She lay beneath him, stunned, trembling while he proceeded swiftly, almost perfunctorily to his release.

When he had finished, he lay still for a long moment, then she heard him say quietly in a voice she barely recognised, 'This—this cannot be endured.'

There was another silence, then he moved, lifting himself away from her and pulling her clothing back into place with a kind of casual indifference that chilled her.

She wanted to be angry—to call him names—to fling something hateful and hurtful at him. Something that would punish him eternally for his shameful treatment of her. But no words would come. Besides, she thought as pain lanced through her, hadn't she insulted him enough? And not just tonight, either?

Hadn't it been her desire to shake his cool arrogance—to wound him that had brought her to this moment in the first place?

Suddenly she felt numb and frightened, as if she was standing on the edge of some abyss. And sad. Above all—sad.

She felt an urge to reach out a hand. Speak his name. But she didn't get the chance. Because Raf spoke first.

'And now get out of my sight, *per favore*.' His voice was harsh as his expression as he stood, refastening his jeans. He did not look at her. 'You said you wished to sleep. *Bene*. Go to bed and do so. You will not be disturbed.'

Emily scrambled to her feet and fled to the stairs. Once in her room, she closed the door, leaning back against its panels, aware of the wild thunder of her heart—and the forlorn ache of her hungry body, trapped in its self-imposed fast.

He'd wanted to seduce her and she'd prevented him. Objective achieved. Job done.

But at what a cost.

It would have been a relief to her feelings if she could have called him a brute—an animal. But it wouldn't have been true. In its way, what he'd done to her had been a demonstration of almost passionless efficiency. There had not been one kiss or caress. Which made it somehow worse.

You prefer to close your heart and mind against me... His words came back to haunt her. Because that was indeed what she'd set out to do from the first, deliberately and precisely. And tonight she'd reaped the bitter harvest of her actions.

This is what you must expect...

Dear God, she thought, was that going to be true? And, if so, how could she bear it?

This could not be how he treated the other women in his life, so she could only hope he would soon grow tired of this sterile and one-sided arrangement. Return to his old ways—old loves, she thought, and flinched.

In the meantime, she couldn't allow herself to be found here brooding like this when Raf came to bed. It was vital not to let him see that anything he might do mattered to her. Or that she might have anything to regret.

She undressed quickly and got into bed, turning her back to the door and thumping the pillow into shape. She wouldn't be asleep when he arrived or, probably, for hours afterwards, but she could pretend. And he'd said he wouldn't disturb her.

And from now on she would keep strictly to her own side of the bed.

It seemed an eternity before she heard him come upstairs and walk past on his way to the bathroom. She burrowed further under the covers, closing her eyes so tightly that tiny stars danced behind her lids, and waited for his return. For the moment when her door would open.

Then, softly but very definitely, Emily heard a very different sound—the subdued click of the spare room door closing just across the passage.

And realised with a sense of shock that, tonight, she would be sleeping entirely alone.

CHAPTER NINE

'I UNDERSTOOD there was going to be a thaw,' Emily muttered to herself, staring defeatedly through the kitchen window.

After three more days there still didn't seem much sign of it. There were flurries of snow most days, and at night the temperature dropped below freezing.

From now on, Emily decided, she would go nowhere without first checking the long-range weather forecast. As well as making sure her destination was entirely her own choice and no one else's, she added wryly.

Today the skies seemed marginally clearer and there was even a wan sun shining intermittently. But if the environment outside the cottage remained bleak, the interior was positively glacial.

She could hardly complain. She'd come to Tullabrae in search of total isolation and for most of the time now she had her wish.

Yet that first night apart from Rafaele had been long and strangely uncomfortable, even though she'd told herself over and over again that this was her greatest victory to date and that, for a few hours at least, she could completely relax.

But it hadn't turned out like that. She'd slept only intermittently and so restlessly that, more than once, she'd woken to find herself on the other side of the bed, lying where his lithe, strong body should have been. Or should not have been, depending on one's point of view.

The scathing words she'd flung at him were still at the forefront of her mind and she'd come downstairs the following morning, determined, if not to apologise, then at least to build some kind of rudimentary bridge between them, only to find the house empty, although the washing-up from the previous evening had been done, the living room fire lit and the log basket filled.

Giving her, she'd realised, biting her lip, something else to feel guilty about.

It had been over two hours before Raf returned and when she'd queried his absence he'd looked at her with faint hauteur.

'I have decided it is time to reconnect with the real world and for that I shall need to use the telephone at the village store. To make calls and wait for answers to them.' He paused. 'Is there a problem?'

'No,' she denied swiftly. 'Of course not. I simply—wondered.'

His mouth curled. 'I should have thought you would simply be relieved.'

In the afternoon he went out again and this time she was careful to ask no questions, least of all when he expected to come back.

And this had become the pattern of their days, with each of his visits to the village seeming to take longer. Or was this because she was becoming increasingly restive on her own?

Yet when he came back the cottage seemed to close in, making her so acutely aware of his presence that she sometimes felt she could hear him breathing. Could sense him near her, their bodies almost brushing.

Although nothing could be further from the truth. Not any more. Because he was scrupulous about maintaining a strict distance between them, especially during the nights, which he continued to spend in the other room. Leaving her in an isolation that suddenly seemed less than splendid.

They still ate together, but any conversation was stilted and his appreciation of the food was coolly and formally expressed. The companionship they'd so briefly discovered had vanished as if it had never existed. And she missed it, she realised in bewilderment. She almost missed the teasing and the tensions his presence engendered. Because the silences were so very much worse.

For her own part, Emily tried to pass as much time as possible in the seclusion of her own room in an attempt to give the impression that her days were full and his absence from them immaterial.

Sometimes she read, at others she worked on one of the jigsaws from the living room cupboard, using an ancient folding table she'd discovered in the cellar and manhandled up the two flights of stairs.

And, quite often, she simply lay on the bed, staring up at the ceiling, trying to plan some way of surviving within the present context of the marriage.

At times she slept a little and this had to be a bonus, because her nights were still troubled and feverish. She could not rest until she heard Raf come upstairs, telling herself she needed the reassurance of knowing he still intended to sleep apart from her.

But, long after his door had safely closed, she found herself wide awake, all too aware that he was lying in the darkness only a few yards away.

There was little doubt that the situation between them was making her increasingly edgy. This morning, the sight of him putting on coat and boots had suddenly needled her.

'Getting ready for your assignation?' she'd asked waspishly.

Raf had looked back at her, brows raised. 'What are you talking about?'

She'd shrugged defensively. 'These endless daily trips. I thought you might have met some bonny Scots lass with a gleam in her eye.'

He'd said coldly, 'Do not talk like a child.' And had gone.

Well, she thought, it hadn't been a wise remark, and she had no excuse for it.

She glanced at her watch. And—no, she wasn't checking on him either, she told herself firmly. Not trying to estimate when he might return. She'd done some washing earlier and put a load into the tumble dryer in the cellar. The cycle was probably over by now and she should empty the drum. All her warm trousers were in there and she was reduced that morning to wearing a cinnamon tweed skirt with a black turtleneck and black wool tights that made her slim legs look longer than ever. Reduced—because looking even remotely female was not part of the plan.

However, female she was, and Raf's casual remark about the possibility of rats in the cellar still lingered unpleasantly in her memory and she always had to steel herself to go down there.

As she turned reluctantly away from the sink to do precisely that she heard a slither and a loud thud and nearly jumped out of her skin.

My God, she thought. Have we lost a chimney?'

She put on her fleece and the frayed wellingtons she'd once sniffed at and went outside to have a look. But there'd been no structural disaster. Instead, a large pile of snow had fallen off the roof and was lying heaped up a few yards away.

And suddenly, nostalgically, she found herself remembering the last time there'd been really heavy snow at the Manor. She'd been eleven, she thought, and she'd run out on to the lawn and built a snowman taller than herself, adorning him in an old beret and a scarf that she'd begged from Penny.

She'd enjoyed looking out of her window each morning to see him standing there like a lopsided sentinel and felt a real sense of loss when the snow melted.

Now she looked at the new drift and grinned.

Raf had called her a child earlier, she thought defiantly. Well, she would totally justify his low opinion. Because it was entirely safer than having him think of her as a woman. If he ever did again…

She began heaping up the snow, grabbing up big handfuls and building them into a substantial column. At first her fingers felt frozen but, as she worked briskly, contact with the snow soon warmed them.

She would never make a sculptor, she decided, as she created broad but unequal shoulders for her figure. Her notion of physique hadn't really improved since she was eleven. But for the first time in days she was actually enjoying herself, humming as she worked.

A large snowball became the head and she fetched small lumps of coal from the bunker for her snowman's eyes and mouth and to make a row of buttons down his front because there were no hats or scarves going spare this time, and, naturally, she didn't wish him to feel undressed.

And she finally completed the effect by fetching a large carrot from the kitchen for his nose, before standing back to regard her handiwork with a critical eye.

'You're a fine figure of a man,' she addressed him aloud and giggled naughtily. 'Or, at least, you could be…'

She removed the carrot from the snowman's head and carefully inserted it in the body instead, placing it at a deliberately jaunty angle down below the row of buttons.

From behind her, Raf said acidly, 'Most artistic.'

She started because she hadn't been aware of his approach, then turned defensively, lifting her chin. He was standing a few feet away, giving the snowman an unsmiling inspection, his dark brows raised. For a moment his coldly sardonic glance brushed her too, then, with a faint shrug, he turned away towards the cottage without another word.

As she watched him go, sudden anger rose within her. She'd been having some harmless fun and he'd spoiled it.

'Humourless bastard,' she hissed under her breath, before snatching up another handful of snow, shaping it into a rough ball and letting him have it, right between the shoulder blades.

Raf stopped dead, then swung back to face her, his face blank with disbelief, while she stared back at him, her eyes glinting with defiance as she realised she'd been wanting to throw things for days.

'Lost for words, *signore*?' she challenged and saw his expression change—slide reluctantly into faint amusement as he looked her up and down, and also something more...

'But certainly not for action, *signora*,' he returned silkily, grabbing up his own handful of snow and advancing on her with obvious purpose.

Being hit by a snowball was one thing, but having it stuffed down her neck as he clearly intended was a totally different matter. And it wasn't going to happen.

She gasped, 'No,' and turned to run, only to find her progress impeded by those clumping boots. Caught completely off balance, she tripped and fell forward into another drift. She wasn't hurt, she wasn't even winded, but she couldn't leap up either and, while she was still struggling, Raf reached her.

'Let go of me.' Her voice was a breathless squeak as he grabbed her, turning her on to her back with almost insulting ease. 'Oh, God, don't you dare...'

'A challenge?' His voice was mocking and that handful of snow was getting dangerously closer, approaching the collar of her sweater as she lay helpless, her dishevelled hair in her eyes and her skirt rucked up to the point of indecency. 'You should know better, *bella mia*.'

She lifted her hands, trying to brace them against his chest, wanting to push him away. Desperate for escape. But found herself instead staring up into his eyes, the breath catching in her throat at what she saw in their depths. Realising that she could not look away.

That, somehow, between one heartbeat and the next, it had become much, much too late.

The handful of snow was discarded and the world shrank, so that there was only the weight of his body against hers, pressing her down into the softness of the drift. And the question in his eyes, demanding an answer.

So that she was no longer trying to free herself. Damp and discomfort were forgotten as her hands slid from his chest to his shoulders and held him, making her own mute demand. Until at last, he bent his head and his mouth took hers with sighing, passionate hunger.

And she was returning his kiss, her lips moving under his, shyly at first, then warmly—eagerly, until, for the first time, they parted in surrender to allow the fierce heat of his tongue to invade the inner sweetness of her mouth.

He gathered her closer in his arms as his kiss deepened endlessly, fiercely, robbing her of breath—of sanity. Of everything but the need to be with him. To know, at last, all that he wanted from her. And to take...

His hand slid under her sweater, seeking the roundness of her breast and brushing aside its covering of lace so that his fingers could caress her nipple into quivering excitement.

Even through the layers of sodden clothing, Emily could feel the hardness of his arousal pressing against her and the swift, scalding flood of her own desire, no longer to be ignored or denied.

When he lifted himself away from her, getting to his feet, she could have moaned with disappointment, but he bent and picked her up in his arms, setting off with her towards the cottage, the oversized boots slipping from her feet to lie forgotten in the snow.

He shouldered his way in, kicking the door shut behind him, then set her down in front of him in her stockinged feet. Near but not touching, he threw off his coat, then began to shed the rest of his clothing, his eyes never leaving hers.

And she was stripping too, her hands clumsy with haste as she dragged wet wool over her head, wrenched at a recalcitrant zip, dealt with the damp cling of tights and underwear.

Naked now, Raf leaned back against the door, holding out his arms, and she ran to him, half-stumbling. He lifted her on to his loins as if she was a leaf on the wind and she sank down on him, gasping, her body on fire with greed as he filled her completely— endlessly, making her achingly aware of every heated, throbbing inch of him.

Instinctively, she found she was lifting her slender legs to fasten round his waist, her hands clamping on his shoulders as he began moving inside her with slow fierce thrusts. Realised, too, that she was discovering her first real response to him, feeding in turn her own sexual appetite. Learning his rhythm— matching it equally in urgency without a thought of denial.

Aware of nothing except his mouth on hers and the deep sensual play of his tongue against hers, and, there—there—at the joining of their bodies, the drive of his hard flesh into her own slick inner wetness, creating sensations deep within her she had never dreamed could exist.

It was heaven. It was hell. It was agony and torment and pleasure beyond belief. A shifting kaleidoscope of feeling where her mind was no longer capable of controlling her body.

Because he musn't stop, she thought as the last semblance of rationality reeled into chaos. *He must never stop.* For, if he did, she would die.

And yet there would be an end. She was aware of it, building up inside from some faint stirrings in the hidden depths of her. Knew, somehow, that it was closing on her, gathering force and pace.

And, as if at some unspoken signal, Raf began to move faster, each stroke even deeper in intensity than the last. Urging her on…

So that, suddenly, it was there, taking her, carrying her away like a great wave rolling in to the shore, and she was clinging to him, her nails scoring his sweat-dampened shoulders, moaning in her throat like an animal in pain as she crashed, shuddering, drowning, into spasm after spasm of pure ecstasy.

As her tightness convulsed gloriously, endlessly around him, Raf's control snapped too and he cried out hoarsely as his body exploded into hers.

When the last, wrenching shiver of pleasure was over and her body had found a kind of peace, Emily slumped forward, sobbing helplessly as she buried her face against his throat. And he held her, murmuring to her in his own language.

Time passed. At some moment, she realised she was being carried across the room and lowered gently, until she felt the softness of the fur rug against her damp skin. Became aware that he was lying beside her, propped on an elbow, his hand gently stroking her body, making her feel as boneless and contented as a purring cat.

Eventually she made herself look at him directly. Tried to read something from the dark, enigmatic face. Attempted to think of something she could say, but failed.

Making him the first one to speak, his fingertips still tracing delicate patterns across her flat stomach. He said quietly, 'So, now we both know, do we not?'

He allowed a significant pause, then added flatly, 'And in future you will never again pretend either to me, or to yourself, that you do not want me. From now on, you share my bed when I wish and you do whatever I desire. *Capisci*?'

Shock lanced through her. He was telling her he'd won, she realised numbly, and, for him, that was all that mattered. Not the rapture she thought they'd shared, which for him would be nothing new. After all, he was probably accustomed to women left mindless and weeping in his arms after lovemaking.

'Yes, I—understand.' Her voice was husky. *I understand only too well*. 'Is that—all you have to say?'

He shrugged a shoulder. 'What do you want to hear? That I knew always there was fire beneath the ice, even if you chose to deny it? And that you were worth waiting for? It is all true.' There was a tinge of mockery in his voice. 'You exceeded my sweetest dreams, *carissima*.'

She didn't really know what she'd hoped he might say. She only knew that he hadn't said it and that there was a small hard pain where her heart should have been.

She said evenly, 'You left out—"for as long as I want".'

'How careless of me.' His tone was light. 'But perhaps I felt the reminder was unnecessary.'

In spite of the fire's warmth, she suddenly felt very cold, so her shiver was involuntary.

She said in a low voice, 'May I get dressed now, please?'

'When you owe me for all the lost pleasure of these past three years?' Raf shook his head almost in derision. 'You have a serious debt to pay, *mia bella*.' His caressing hand moved. Became exquisitely specific. He saw her eyes widening, darkening to emerald, and smiled ironically. 'And, now that we have both recovered a little, I shall expect the next instalment very soon,' he added softly, and bent, taking one dusky rose nipple gently between his lips and bringing it to throbbing arousal with the delicate flicker of his tongue.

She'd have given all she possessed to turn away from him. To revert to her former indifference. But it was far too late for that. And, it seemed, he hadn't been fooled anyway.

Besides, deep inside her, impossibly, incredibly, she already felt the inexorable tug of renewed desire.

Raf raised his head and looked at her. He said quite gently, '*Precisamente*. And I think, don't you, *cara*, that we would both be more comfortable if we pursued this matter in bed.'

He got lithely to his feet and extended his hand to her. She allowed his fingers to clasp hers, to draw her upwards. For a moment, he stood looking down at her and Emily lowered her lashes, letting them veil the welter of confusion in her eyes.

She thought he was going to speak, but he said nothing. Instead, he simply led her to the stairs and she went without protest, feeling her heartbeat quicken in an excitement and need that she was unable to control.

Wanting to die of shame, yet knowing, at the same time, that she was already far beyond it.

Because her body was now his, irrevocably, and for all time. And there was nothing she could do to change that, even though she knew the time would inevitably come when he would want her no longer.

Then, as the bed received them and Raf took her in his arms, whispering her name against her eager mouth, all thinking stopped.

The bath water was warm and deep and Emily sank into it gratefully. She felt drained and hollow, but, then, why wouldn't she after such a prolonged and intense lesson in the physical aspects of lovemaking? she asked herself wryly.

Even now the merest recall of what had happened during the past few hours brought the blood soaring to her face.

She'd never imagined she could be capable of such abandonment, or that she could be brought over and over again to such a pitch of frantic, exquisite delight.

Even to someone of her inexperience, it was clear that Raf had been incredibly generous and unselfish with her, deliberately restraining his own satisfaction until hers had been achieved.

As, she realised, he would have done from the beginning—if she'd allowed it.

But that, of course, was the secret of his success with women, Emily thought, flinching. And something she needed to keep at the forefront of her mind—the knowledge that she was far from the first to experience the sublime magic of his hands and mouth on her skin, or the controlled male power of him sheathed inside her as he took her to the next rapturous pinnacle.

And as she'd floated slowly back to reality, she'd heard him praising her softly, telling her how wonderful she was and how beautiful. How she was his one desire.

Which, of course, was not the truth—not any of it, and she would be a fool to believe it—or even hope that it could be so.

But what was one more folly amongst so many others?

She'd left Raf sleeping, because, in spite of her own exhaustion, her mind was too restless to let her claim any kind of oblivion beside him.

She'd paused for a moment at the side of the bed, looking down at him, his long lashes dark on his cheek, the firmness of his mouth relaxed into a half-smile.

How could she ever have thought she didn't want him? she wondered sadly.

The temptation to bend and kiss him was almost overwhelming, but she controlled it, telling herself that he deserved his rest, and, instead, slipped quietly away to bathe and wash her hair.

To make herself beautiful again for her lover, she thought ironically, as if she'd ever been more than reasonably attractive. She had no illusions. She'd seen the thinly veiled surprise in people's faces when she'd been introduced as his wife. Had heard the unspoken question: What does he see in her?

Well, a challenge was the answer to that, she thought. But a challenge that didn't exist any more, leaving her nowhere to hide—not now she'd given herself in total surrender.

Yet wasn't that what she'd always feared? she asked herself, her throat tightening. Why she'd tried so desperately to keep him at a distance? Because she'd feared from the first that she would lose herself—her identity—any vestige of independence—in so total a belonging?

Not that he saw it that way. *A serious debt…* His words.

And when that debt was paid, what then?

She submerged abruptly and came up gasping. Well, she knew the answer to that. She'd be 'let go' in the classic phrase that meant she'd become redundant—surplus to requirements. Unnecessary in the cruelest way.

She'd been warned, of course. Raf had told her that he would make her want him, but that he'd show her no mercy when it happened.

And I was so sure, she thought, *that I could prove him wrong.*

She got out of the bath and dried herself, then rubbed the worst of the moisture from her hair and brushed it on to her shoulders.

Raf's robe was hanging on the back of the bathroom door and, acting on impulse, she put it on. The scent of his cologne still lingered in the folds of silk and she drew a deep breath, allowing herself a moment of sensuous reminiscence as she secured the sash round her slender waist.

At the foot of the stairs she halted, looking round the living room, which was far from its usual pristine state. The fire had died long ago and there were sofa cushions scattered on the floor, along with their discarded clothing.

And a strange sound in the quietness too. The noise, she realized, of raindrops beating against the window. The promised thaw was here. And had been for hours, judging from the way the banks of snow were rapidly turning to slush.

I never realised, she thought, and her mouth curved into a reluctant grin. But, in Raf's arms, I probably wouldn't have noticed if one of these mountains had turned into Mount Etna on a bad day.

And we can leave. If we want to. Yet perhaps I'd rather stay. Let the honeymoon go on.

She wandered into the kitchen and filled the kettle. She'd just put it on the stove when she heard the sound of an approaching vehicle and saw Angus's Jeep coming up the track, melting snow spraying from its tyres.

'Oh, hell,' Emily muttered and flew into the living room, snatching up sweaters, jeans, underwear and her skirt and pushing them behind the sofa, before replacing its cushions. Giving the place at least a façade of respectability.

By the time Angus reached the door she had it open and was smiling brightly if breathlessly. 'Oh, hi.'

His own expression was dour. Raf's robe covered her from throat to ankles, but she still sensed disapproval. He was carrying her discarded wellingtons.

'I found these outside.'

'Oh.' She took them from him. 'Well, thank you.'

'Are you not feeling well?'

Clearly, only being stricken by a passing virus could account for being in a dressing gown at this time of day.

'I'm fine.' Emily shrugged. 'Just thought I'd—wash my hair.'

Clearly such eccentric behaviour was beyond him. He produced a sheaf of papers from an inside pocket of his parka. 'Auntie asked me to bring these up to your man. They're the answers to the emails he sent this morning. He usually comes down for them in the afternoon, so she was a wee bit concerned.'

'You mean there's a computer at the shop?'

'Well, you should know,' Angus said. 'You must have made your booking on it.'

Emily bit her lip. 'Why, yes, of course. I was forgetting.' She paused. 'But surely it belongs to your aunt. It can't be for general use.'

'Your husband's a friend of Mrs Albero, and she was a Lomax before she got married, it seems, so Auntie Maggie was prepared to make a concession. Besides, he pays well enough for the privilege. And she says he must have money to burn, the time he spends on the phone to Italy.' He looked past her into the cottage. 'Is he not around?'

'He's not available at the moment,' she said evasively, trying not to blush and praying that Raf would not make a liar of her by suddenly appearing stark naked and all too available.

'Then I'd best give them to you.' He handed her the papers. 'They're mostly in Italian, you'll find.' He produced a separate sheet. 'And here are his phone messages. He's been waiting for these.'

As Emily took the sheet, she glanced casually down at the list of names and froze as one seemed to leap out at her. And not once, but three times. *Valentina.*

There was a sudden roaring in her ears and she felt the world recede to some far distance as a small despairing voice in her head whispered silently, Oh, no—please. Surely not...

Yet what else had she expected? she asked herself numbly. She'd had sex with Raf—nothing more. He'd required recompense for her insult to his masculinity and had taken it in full measure. But he'd made no promises. Had offered no long-term commitment or guarantees of fidelity. On the contrary.

He still planned to live his life on his own terms, and she was a fool if she imagined otherwise.

Angus's voice reached her on a note of impatience. 'I said— I suppose you'll be leaving soon.'

She looked at him almost blankly. 'I—I don't know what the plans are.'

'Well, your man told Auntie he'd need to be returning to Rome as soon as the weather improved, and they reckon the snow will be all gone by morning.'

He's not my man. She wanted to shriek the words aloud. I may belong to him now, she thought, but he's not mine and he never will be.

She became aware that he was watching her, his face slightly puzzled. He said rather more gently, 'It's a shame you haven't had the chance to get out and about more during your stay. It's very beautiful round here.' He paused. 'Maybe you'll come back some time.'

'Perhaps,' she said. 'Who knows?'

She watched him trudge back to the Jeep, then lifted her hand in farewell as she closed the door.

She folded the list and put it inside the emails. Her pride

demanded that Raf shouldn't know that she'd seen it, although he probably wouldn't care. She'd noticed some envelopes in a box with writing paper in the cupboard beside the fireplace and she fetched one of them and tucked all the paperwork inside, sealing down the flap.

Then she collected the armful of clothing from behind the sofa and took it all upstairs.

Raf was awake and sitting up yawning and pushing his hair out of his eyes when she entered the bedroom. He looked at her, absorbing what she was wearing, and his smile almost stopped her heart.

'So there you are, *mia bella*,' he said softly. 'I missed you.'

'I thought you'd still be asleep.' She busied herself sorting out their clothing.

He shrugged a shoulder. 'Something woke me. An engine, perhaps?'

'Probably.' She paused. 'Angus McEwen was here.'

He stilled. His eyes went over her again, this time without amusement, as if he was assessing the cling of the silk against her body.

'*Perche?*' he rapped out. 'For what reason?'

'He brought you this.' She walked over to the bed and handed him the envelope. 'Emails and stuff. You didn't turn up to collect them and his aunt thought they might be urgent.'

'If you remember,' he said slowly, 'I had other far more urgent matters to attend to.' He captured her wrist, pulling her down on the bed beside him. 'And I think it is time I took back my robe,' he added, reaching for the sash.

She wriggled away, her answering smile faintly fixed. 'I need to extend the loan for a little while longer,' she told him lightly. 'The kettle will be boiling and I have coffee to make.'

But by the time she'd made it Raf was already downstairs, fully dressed and pulling on his parka. His face was sombre, even frowning, and a renewal of passion was clearly the last thing on his mind.

The envelope, she saw, was sticking out of his pocket.

He said without preamble, 'I am going to make travel arrangements, Emilia, to return to Rome. I hope to leave in the morning. Can you be ready by then?'

So Valentina only has to crook her little finger…

Pain slashed at her but she managed to say brightly, 'Yes, of course. If you can take me to the station, I still have the return portion of my train ticket.'

He was at the door, but turned abruptly, his frown deepening. 'Train?' he repeated. 'What are you talking about?'

'You're going to Italy,' she said. 'And I—I can go home.'

'*Certamente*, but to my house in Rome, not your English sanctuary.' His tone brooked no argument. 'You are my wife and your place is with me. Nowhere else.'

'But—surely…' she began, then halted.

'Surely—what?' He glanced at his watch, impatient to be off. 'There is something more you wish to say?'

Yes, she thought. But where to begin?

She bent her head. 'It doesn't matter.'

'I think perhaps it does, but there is no time now.' All the same, he came across to her, his hand cupping her chin, turning her face up to his as his mouth came down on hers in a deep, hard, lingering kiss that made her entire body clench in trembling desire.

When he released her, he was smiling crookedly.

'Later,' he whispered. Then he was gone and, as the cottage door banged shut behind him, Emily stood, her fingers touching the faint tenderness of her lips.

He still wanted her, she thought, so he was taking her with him. Yet she had no exclusive rights to him. Because, in Rome, his beautiful Valentina was also waiting to stake her claim.

As she stared unseeingly into space, it occurred to her that the kiss, which had just left her breathless and melting, might simply have been the beginning of a very long goodbye.

CHAPTER TEN

NEXT day, Emily found herself on a plane bound for Rome, under the confused impression she'd just been caught up in a whirlwind.

The first time she'd travelled with Raf had been immediately after their wedding, when she'd still been too stunned by her father's loss, and too shocked to find that she was actually married to this comparative stranger, to pay much heed to the arrangements for the journey.

Now she had plenty of time to appreciate how smoothly things ran when their wheels were oiled by money. How transfers were accomplished, formalities reduced to a minimum and first class seats on aircraft suddenly became available.

But it also brought home to Emily just how little control she now had over her own life.

A life already occupied by another woman. Someone who was never really out of Raf's thoughts, even while he was seducing me. Someone he can hardly wait to return to. Valentina…

She moved suddenly, restively, and he glanced at her. 'Is something wrong?

'I was just wondering—will I be able to send for my clothes?'

His brows lifted. 'Why?'

'Because I can't manage with the few things I took to Scotland.'

'You will not have to do so.' He paused. 'They can be thrown away and I shall tell Signora Penistone to dispose of the rest of your wardrobe in England.' He smiled at her, adding softly, 'And tomorrow I will take you shopping.'

'But that's totally unnecessary. I'd prefer my own things.'

'They belong to the past, Emilia. You are no longer a child hiding in the country, but my wife, the Contessa Di Salis, and you will dress accordingly.'

'But being your wife is a strictly temporary arrangement,' she said in a low voice. 'As it always was. And the fact that we—we now have sex doesn't change a thing.'

'Does it not?' There was a harsh note in his voice. 'I thought perhaps it might do so, but I see that was foolish of me.'

No, she thought, not looking at him. I was supposed to be the fool—duped into passivity—into ecstatic acceptance by a few hours of expert lovemaking.

For a moment she found herself remembering the previous night. How unexpectedly, sublimely gentle he'd been with her, as if he'd sensed her mental tensions and had wished to calm them. How he'd seemed to be aware of her every breath—each flicker of her eyelashes, as he'd led her, slowly and patiently, to the sweet tumult of orgasm, then held her close as she slept, so that she'd woken this morning, still in his arms.

But then that was one of his undoubted gifts, she thought fiercely. To make every woman he slept with feel as if she was uniquely desirable—and desired.

'Nevertheless you will dress in future to suit your status,' he went on. 'And also to please me. Which is why I intend to supervise your purchases in person. However, you may retain what you are wearing at present,' he added, his eyes resting on the cinammon skirt she was travelling in. His mouth twisted sardonically. 'It has—memories I treasure.'

Among so many others, she thought, her heart twisting, and none of them to do with me.

Hypocrite—*hypocrite*…

She said quietly, 'As you wish.' She paused. 'What are people going to think, do you suppose, when you suddenly turn up with me, after three years of living as a virtual bachelor?' *Above all, what is Valentina Colona going to think? And how can you do this to her?*

'People?' he queried curtly. 'People may think what they wish. Their opinions do not trouble me.'

What supreme arrogance. Her voice shook. 'But not the whole truth, either—as we both know.' And could have bitten her tongue.

He said slowly, 'You talk in riddles, *mia cara*. What is that supposed to mean?'

She shrugged evasively. 'Just that—everyone has to answer to someone in this life, *signore*. Even you.'

'Perhaps,' he said. 'I decided long ago to answer only to myself.'

Emily bit her lip. 'And that's why I'm being suddenly dragged back to Italy, where I can't even speak the language?'

'I will arrange lessons for you.'

'I hardly imagine I'll be there long enough to justify the expense.'

'But an ability to speak a foreign language is always an asset.' His smile grazed her skin. 'Now, if you will excuse me, I have work I must do.' And he took some papers from his briefcase.

Emily stared out of the plane window. So, here she was, she thought, the Contessa Di Salis—but this time in fact instead of the usual polite fiction. Yet she still didn't believe it, and knew it would take much more than first class travel and a wardrobe full of designer labels to convince her that this new identity was really hers.

Besides, everyone she met in Rome would know about Valentina Colona, and she was bound to suffer from the inevitable comparisons that would be made. A skinny redhead, she thought, up against one of the world's most sophisticated women.

Except I don't want to compete, she acknowledged painfully. Not when I know I've already lost.

And realised how strange it was that she should suddenly be thinking in terms of loss rather than anticipating the freedom from her marriage that she'd always craved.

She looked down at her hand, watching the glint of the sapphire ring she was wearing once again.

To her surprise, Raf had suddenly produced it before they'd left for the airport, saying quietly, 'I found this with your wedding ring, Emilia. In future, I expect you to wear it—*per favore*'.

Her face had warmed as she remembered its significance, but, taking one look at the implacable set of his firm mouth, she'd reluctantly swallowed back her instinctive protest. Mutely, she'd held out her hand and let him place the ring on her finger, then, still in silence, had walked out to the car.

But what would become of the ring—and of her—when his

desire eventually waned? she wondered. What hell of loneliness might be waiting then? And her mind shivered away from the prospect.

At the same time, she knew she should be more concerned with the immediate future and her introduction to a life for which she knew she was woefully unprepared. A life that might call for the kind of painful discoveries and reluctant compromises she couldn't even imagine as yet. Where she would need to be blind, deaf and dumb in order to survive.

But, for now, there was the comfort of a first class seat to enjoy, glossy magazines to flick through and champagne to drink. Who could ask for more? she thought ironically, stealing a sideways glance at Raf, his dark face absorbed and intent as he made notes in the margin of some document.

He did not turn his head, but, as if aware of her scrutiny, he replaced the papers and pen in his case and reached silently for her hand, raising it swiftly and gently to his lips. Then kept it clasped firmly in his as the descent to Rome was announced.

And Emily, looking down at the strong brown fingers interlaced with hers, suddenly felt her heart miss a beat and her breathing falter.

It didn't mean anything, she assured herself. He probably thought she was nervous about the plane landing, and she was—grateful. That was all. Wasn't it? *Wasn't it?*

Only to hear, from nowhere, a small, desperate voice in her head whispering—begging, Hold my hand always—please. Never let me go, darling—*darling*.

For a moment, shock seized her by the throat. Overwhelmed her. Rendering her breathless. Powerless.

Leaving her to wonder how it could have taken such a simple gesture to make her understand that she was in love with him. Deeply and passionately in love.

A love, she thought, stunned, that had probably begun a much longer time ago than she dared to remember, or admit, even to herself.

A love that she had tried with all her strength to deny for three whole years.

But failed.

Impossible now to pinpoint the day, moment, hour when Rafaele Di Salis had first put his seal on her. She could only recognise that it had happened. And find some way to live with it.

I told myself I disliked him, she realised with anguish, because I was too scared to examine how he really made me feel. And too young to deal with it, anyway.

I didn't want to belong to anyone as completely as I knew I would to him, because I thought I wasn't ready for that. Didn't want to become part of his life—flesh of his flesh, bone of his bone, because even then I knew somehow that Raf could have the power to destroy me if I came too close.

So it was infinitely easier to focus on Simon. To convince myself that *he* was the one, instead of a mere adolescent crush, and use him to try to put Raf out of my mind.

Only it hadn't worked, she thought wretchedly. And when Simon had gone, she had had to learn to distance herself from Raf in other ways, out of sheer self-preservation.

So she'd deliberately and consistently driven him away, then told herself she was indifferent when he'd sought comfort elsewhere—even though, in reality, she'd been torn apart, suffering the torments of the damned through jealousy.

She touched the tip of her tongue to suddenly dry lips.

And her sole certainty of survival had been to ensure the marriage existed in name only.

Yet, with victory in sight, she'd engineered her own downfall by that crazy demand for an annulment.

My quite deliberate mistake, she thought.

Because instinct had told her that Raf would not allow such an insult to his virility simply to pass.

Which meant that everything that had happened between them since was entirely her own fault, she thought soberly. And she had no one but herself to blame if she now had to endure the consequences.

Leaving her with no choice but to go on keeping her terrible secret, while her marriage to Raf ran its brief course, and the inevitable moment arrived when he would send her away.

And there's nothing I can do about it, she thought, with shuddering anguish. Nothing. Except prepare myself for the heartbreak that I've always dreaded. And pretend all over again that it doesn't matter.

And all this just because he took my hand—and held it…

The skies were grey over Rome and rain was falling in a steady downpour. Emily sat stiffly at Raf's side, watching the drops beat against the windows of the car which was taking them to the house they would share for—what? Weeks—months? Certainly not years, she thought, sinking her teeth into her lower lip, tasting panic like acid in her throat as she contemplated what lay ahead of her.

Oh God, she thought, how could I possibly have allowed this to happen?

His voice reached her. 'You are very quiet, *mia bella*. Are you tired?'

'A little—perhaps.'

It wasn't true. She was just sick at heart and bewildered, totally unprepared for the unwelcome revelation of her true feelings for him. And at a loss to know how to deal with them.

'I have had some work done to the house,' he said after a pause. 'I hope it will meet with your approval. I have spent so little time there myself over the past years, that I did not realise how dark it might seem, or how dismal.'

To a stranger… The words were unspoken, but they nevertheless seemed to hover in the air between them.

But she could hardly object. A stranger under his roof was all she was—or ever would be. And she must never forget that.

Raf was speaking again. 'If there are any further changes you wish to make, you must tell me, *naturalmente*.'

I don't care about dark or dismal. I'd live in a hole in the ground if you only loved me…

Aloud, she said jerkily, 'No, I'm sure it will be—beautiful.' She forced a smile. 'I can't wait to see it.'

'I regret that I cannot be there when you pass judgement,' he said. 'But, once I have seen you safely to the house, I must return to my office in the city.'

'You're leaving me on my own—on our first day back?' The query jerked from her before she could prevent it. Oh, God, she thought in horror, how needy and pathetic did that sound?

'Unfortunately, it is unavoidable. I have an essential meeting, and other urgent matters to attend to.'

Valentina Colona among them?

She dared not ask it aloud. Instead she lifted her chin and said, 'Of course. I—understand perfectly.'

And waited for the knife to turn inside her as it inevitably did.

Raf's mouth twisted. 'I do not think that is altogether the truth, *mia cara*. Please believe that I do not wish to leave you.'

'I've told you. It's—absolutely fine.'

'No,' he said. 'Plainly, it is not.' His arm went round her, drawing her close, his fingers cupping her breast under her coat. 'Now, what can I do to make amends, *mi amore*?' His other hand captured her chin, turning her face up to his so that he could kiss her mouth. As her lips parted beneath his, she became aware too of his thumb stroking her nipple to helpless throbbing life even through the thickness of her sweater.

'Raf!' She pulled back her head, her whisper strained— breathless. 'Stop this. Your driver—he'll see.'

His own voice was low and husky. 'The glass between us is a screen, *carissima*. I promise he will see nothing.' His hand slid under the hem of her skirt, caressing her knee, as he kissed her again, his tongue achingly, warmly sensuous against hers.

She tried to think of some protest that would halt this scandalous—this *impossible* torment right here and now, but Raf's fingers were moving, edging slowly, enticingly upwards and Emily discovered, shocked, that her entire being was suddenly focused with shivering, burning excitement on the totally inevitable. On where he was going to touch her next—and precisely how…

She was already beyond speech, or even coherent thought.

His hand moulded her through her underclothing, claiming her, and she gasped soundlessly, arching towards him, as his fingertips began to caress her, gently pushing aside the barriers of fabric to discover the moist white-heat of desire that he'd created. Lingering there.

Then slowly allowing the expert glide of his touch to seek her tiny, sensitive bud and stroke it to a peak of aching, aroused delight. Holding her with almost cruel precision, on the supreme, burning edge of release, until she whimpered into his mouth, pleading wordlessly for the promised pleasure.

And, at last, when her fainting senses thought they could endure no more, he took her over the brink into the fierce, shuddering contractions of satiation, stifling her breathless moans with his lips.

Only brief moments later, still speechless and trembling, Emily became dimly aware that the car was slowing to a halt, turning through high wrought iron gates on to a broad drive. Signalling that they had arrived at the house and making her realise at the same time that Raf had gauged her ascent to rapture with a deliberate and wicked accuracy that, in retrospect, made her burn with shame and embarrassment.

As the car drew up outside the imposing main entrance, Emily saw Gaspare hovering with a large umbrella, his smile warm if faintly anxious.

'A hundred welcomes, *Eccelenza*, and to you, *Vossignoria*,' he greeted them, bowing. 'We are so happy to see you again.'

Emily's legs were still shaking under her as she left the car, but she managed to smile and say, '*Grazie*.'

She was aware of Raf taking her arm and wanted to pull away, but it was impossible because Gaspare was holding the umbrella protectively over them both as they went up the wide steps and into the house.

'Shall I have coffee brought to the *salotto, Eccelenza*?'

'The Contessa is tired from the journey,' Raf said smoothly. 'I think we would both prefer to go to our rooms and rest for a while. Come, *cara*.'

Face burning, she allowed herself to be conducted unwillingly up the imposing staircase and along the gallery to the massive double doors at the end which led to the master suite.

In spite of her anger and humiliation, she recognised instantly that the main bedroom had been transformed. The walls were freshly painted and sheer ivory drapes hung at the windows and curtained the enormous bed.

But this did nothing to appease her, especially when she turned on him and saw that he was locking the door.

'What the hell are you doing?' she demanded furiously.

'You seem upset, *carissima*,' Raf drawled. 'If you have something to say to me, I would prefer it to be in total privacy.'

'I have something to say all right.' She drew a breath. 'How dare you treat me like that?' Her voice was uneven. 'Manipulate me. As if I was some—cheap plaything.'

He was walking to her, but he halted, the dark brows snapping together. 'If that is how it seemed to you,' he said, 'then you must forgive me. It was certainly not my intention.'

'Then what did you mean by it?'

His mouth twisted. 'I thought—to give you some pleasure, *mia bella*.'

'You imagined I wanted to be—used—humiliated?'

'No,' he said. 'That did not occur to me.' He paused, then added drily, 'But I see now I made a mistake. I was misled by your response, *carissima*. You hid your reluctance well.'

His jibe was deserved and she knew it as her colour deepened and she looked away, mortified. 'I hate you.' Her voice was husky, her body still throbbing from the exquisite anguish so recently inflicted on her.

'*Per me va benissimo, cara*.' His tone was mocking. 'That is fine with me. But keep your hatred for the daylight hours, *e chiaro*. I have other plans for your nights.'

'But for how long?' She spread her hands in angry appeal. 'How many nights will there be until I'm no longer a novelty?'

Raf shrugged off his jacket and began to unfasten his tie. '*Chissà*! Who knows?' he countered. 'For me, at this time, *mi amore*, you are like an undiscovered country, possessing all the charm of the unknown.' He gave her a sardonic look. 'But you will be relieved to know I have no long term strategies that need concern you. Your torture will end—eventually.'

'Then make it now,' she said passionately. 'Let me go back to England, and you go on with your—your real life here.' She flung her head back. 'However much you once owed my father, it could never justify being forced to live like this. You must see that. So don't let's have anything else to regret. Just consider the debt paid in full, and let me—go home.'

'It is not a question of money,' he said quietly, unbuttoning his shirt. 'It never was. As for regrets—I have only one. That I did not pay court to you as I should have done before our marriage. Taught you a little about your body and its needs, so that you would have welcomed me into your bed on our wedding night, instead of treating me as if I was a monster.

'But it is useless to wish the past away,' he added. 'And I have no intention of letting you go. You are my wife, Emilia, and, while you remain so, this is now your home. And, to make quite certain you do not forget that, we shall consummate our marriage all over again, here and now, in this room and this bed.'

'But you can't.' Her voice sounded hoarse. 'You have work—meetings to go to. You—you said so.'

He shrugged. 'All that can wait. Because I have a far more pressing appointment with you, *mia cara sposa*.' His tone was faintly jeering. 'However, I will make sure those involved are well compensated for any inconvenience.' He sent her a sardonic look. 'And you also, *mia bella*, as it is daytime and I am intruding on your right to seclusion.'

'I want nothing from you!'

'No?' Raf shed the rest of his clothes with unhurried grace and stretched out on the bed, his naked skin golden in the subdued light. He beckoned to her. 'Then come here, my lovely one,' he commanded softly. 'And prove that to me.' He smiled at her. 'If you can.'

When Emily eventually awoke it was late afternoon and Raf had been gone for hours. She had a vague memory, as she'd lain half-dozing, spent and languid from the passion she'd been unable to resist, of his hand stroking her cheek, his lips touching her hair as he'd left her.

Not that it excused, even for a moment, the way he'd treated her, she thought, turning over and burying her hot face in the pillow, as she remembered the way she'd been reduced to frantic, sobbing abandonment in his arms in spite of her protests.

And knowing that she loved him made it even more difficult and hurtful to acknowledge that her only attraction for him was a physical one.

That there would never be more than sex on offer in this marriage, and any deeper fulfilment would always be denied her.

For Rafaele, she told herself painfully, love was not an option. And she had to accept that and hope for nothing more.

She was suddenly aware that there was movement in the room and sat up, startled. A plump girl whom she'd never seen before was crossing towards the dressing room, carrying Emily's discarded clothing over her arm.

'*Un momento*.' Emily hastily hitched up the fine linen sheet to cover her bare breasts. 'Who are you, please? And where are you going with those?'

The girl swung round defensively. She had a round, stolid face and eyes so dark they looked almost black. Unsmiling, she bobbed a curtsy. 'I am Apollonia. I am here to wait on *vossignoria*.'

Oh, God, thought Emily, her heart sinking. This must be the maid Raf threatened me with. I didn't think he was serious. But here she is and I really need her tiptoeing about, picking up the clothes he's taken off me, like I want a hole in the head.

She said quite gently, 'But I haven't asked for anyone, Apollonia. Perhaps you should have waited until you were sent for.'

Apollonia's mouth pursed into a button and she almost shrugged. '*Lo stesso, eccomi, signora*. So perhaps I may make ready a bath for you?'

Emily hesitated, tempted to tell the girl that she was perfectly capable of filling her own tub. Especially as it just involved turning on a pair of taps rather than running about with great pans of hot water, she thought, with a pang of memory.

But the maid was only doing her job, she reminded herself. And, until she had a chance to speak to Rafaele that evening and explain that she didn't wish to be waited on, she supposed, in fairness, she should let her get on with it.

On the other hand, she had no wish to get out of bed, naked, in front of a po-faced stranger.

She said, 'Very well, Apollonia. A bath would be good. And perhaps you could find me a robe.'

The girl did not return her smile. 'You will wish to dress for dinner, *signora*. What may I bring you to wear?'

'I'm afraid there isn't much choice. Most of my clothes are in England.' *And probably on their way to the charity shop, even as we speak.* She added, 'Just—do your best for this evening.'

Apollonia nodded in acquiescence, but there was no lightening in her expression. She went to the dressing room and returned with a towelling robe that Emily guessed belonged to Raf.

The bath was wonderful, deep and scented, and when she came back into the bedroom, after a prolonged and luxurious soaking, she found fresh underwear on the bed, with a charcoal pleated skirt and a plain white sweater in thin wool. The maid herself, mercifully, was nowhere to be seen.

Once dressed, Emily took a long look at herself. Neat, she thought, but not spectacular. And now she had to go downstairs, knowing that the entire household must be aware exactly how the Count had celebrated his wife's return to his home.

But there were no sly smiles or knowing looks from anyone, least of all Gaspare, who was waiting eagerly to open the doors to the *salotto* for her.

There'd been a transformation in this room too. The heavier pieces of furniture had been replaced by elegant antiques from a much earlier era and most of the gloomy portraits in their ornate frames had also vanished from the newly painted walls. The cavernous leather seats had gone too, exchanged for deeply cushioned sofas, upholstered in a rich cream fabric.

There was a cheerful blaze in the great stone fireplace, she saw, and coffee already waiting, with a plate of the small sweet biscuits made with honey and nuts that she'd liked so much on her previous visit. Rosanna, the cook, must have somehow remembered after all this time, she thought, her throat tightening suddenly.

'It is good? My lady approves?' Gaspare's tone was faintly worried. He gestured around him. 'Before—too dark—too sad, I think.'

'It's all wonderful,' she said, and meant it. He wanted reassurance, she thought, that she liked the change in her surroundings. That she was going to be comfortable, so that she'd stay. He didn't understand it wasn't a question of new décor, and never had been.

And she couldn't tell him.

But no doubt everything would become perfectly clear in due course—when her replacement moved in.

And, talking of replacements…

'Gaspare.' She detained him as he was about to leave the room. 'The girl Apollonia—is she new?'

'*Si, signora*. But her recommendations are good, although, in the past, she has worked mainly for ladies who are widows and not young.' He looked anxious. 'This is advancement for her and she wishes to please.'

You could have fooled me, Emily thought drily, but she said only, '*Grazie,* Gaspare. I was interested, that's all.'

She was pouring some coffee when she heard the loud peal of a bell and a moment later Gaspare returned, looking much more cheerful.

'The Signora Albero asks if she can be received, my lady.'

'Why, yes, of course.' Emily scrambled to her feet. 'And bring another cup, will you, Gaspare?'

Fiona Albero was a pretty girl, with curling brown hair and blue eyes that sparked with mischief. She looked stunning in a honey-coloured wool suit and an enormous diamond glittered like an iceberg in the sun on her wedding finger.

'It's so good to see you again,' she said, her voice still carrying a hint of her Scottish ancestry. She grasped both Emily's hands in hers. 'But please don't pretend you remember me,' she added, her mouth curving humorously. 'Marcello and I agreed you were operating on autopilot the night we met. You looked totally poleaxed—as I suppose anyone would if they woke up and found themselves married to Rafaele.

'Don't get me wrong,' she went on hurriedly. 'He's Marcello's best friend since they were at school, and he's absolutely terrific—kind and generous as well as totally gorgeous. But it occurs to me that he could also be—formidable.'

Emily smiled back. 'It's occurred to me too,' she said calmly. 'Won't you sit down?'

'Raf suggested I should call round,' Fiona went on when they were both drinking coffee. 'I said it was too soon, but he seemed to think you might be feeling a tad—uprooted. Which I would totally understand, having been through it.'

'It has been something of a shock to the system,' Emily admitted wryly.

'But it's marvellous that you're here at last.' Fiona looked around her and nodded. 'And he's done wonders with the house. It's always seemed so sad and empty in the past. Small wonder to me that he's always preferred his apartment in the city.'

Is there one? thought Emily. I didn't know.

But she didn't say so aloud. Instead, 'I thought the cottage at Tullabrae was delightful.'

'Did you?' Fiona looked very pleased. 'It's where my father was born and we use it a lot, but not in the winter, of course,' she added with a shiver. 'I tried to talk Raf out of it, believe me. Said if he wanted to take you on a second honeymoon, the Bahamas would be a safer bet, but he was adamant. And here you are, so maybe it works its magic all the year round.'

She paused. 'Did he cook for you while you were there?'

Emily stared at her. 'Raf can cook?' she asked in astonishment.

Fiona rolled her eyes expressively. 'He's one of these seriously aggravating men who can throw a few ingredients into a pan and come up with a gourmet meal.' She gave a naughty giggle. 'But maybe—on honeymoon—he had better ways of spending his time.'

She saw Emily flush and looked remorseful. 'Oh, Lord, now I've embarrassed you. My big mouth. I'm really sorry.'

'No, really. It's fine,' Emily hastened to assure her. 'Besides, I suspect I may need to grow an extra skin or two, anyway over the next few weeks.' She hesitated. 'You must have wondered…'

'No,' Fiona said instantly, then pulled a face. 'Well, yes, we have—naturally. I mean—to be honest—when we first saw you, we couldn't get over how very young you seemed to be coping with marriage—especially to someone like Raf.'

Emily bit her lip. 'But I didn't cope,' she said quietly. 'Not even marginally.' She paused. 'Has he never said…?'

'He's said nothing. And, frankly, we've never dared ask.' Fiona smiled ruefully. 'Raf doesn't encourage speculation about his private life, not even when he and Marcello have been off on one of their lads' hunting trips to Umbria. And I'm not here to probe either.'

She looked a trifle awkward. 'Of course, when Raf mentioned a second honeymoon, we did hope that things might have changed.' She shook her head. 'He's always seemed so—alone.'

Emily looked away. 'Please,' she said with difficulty, 'you don't have to spare my feelings. I'm under no illusion about his—lifestyle. And Raf's never pretended that he's been—lonely.'

There was a silence, then Fiona said gently, 'I don't think we're talking about the same thing at all. But, as I have no right to be discussing this anyway, I'll shut up and leave you in peace.'

She reached for her bag. 'I just wanted to welcome you, and to let you know I'm only a phone call away. I also know a good language teacher when you decide to take the plunge, and it helps, believe me. Besides, I think Raf would really appreciate it if you did learn Italian.

'We'll give you a few days to find your feet,' she added buoyantly. 'Then we'll be pestering you to have dinner with us.'

She smiled warmly, gave Emily a reassuring pat and vanished as quickly as she'd arrived.

Emily spent the rest of the day exploring the entire house and noting all the changes that had been made. They must have taken a long time, she thought, and Raf had clearly begun them when he was still intending to divorce her.

So they weren't planned for my sake, she thought unhappily, but for someone very different.

He hadn't stinted anywhere either, she told herself as she stood in the dining room, admiring the expertly restored frescos.

The whole place seemed infinitely lighter and even more spacious than she remembered. It was as if heavy shutters had suddenly been flung back, allowing the sunlight to pour into a dark and shadowed room.

I could have been so happy here, if only...

Tears tightened her throat, but she swallowed them back resolutely.

Because there was no point in wishing for what she could not have. Or in regretting that when Raf had come to her bedroom on that night three years ago she'd not been able to overcome her nervousness and total lack of confidence enough to smile at him—or hold out her hand. Or say—something—anything—however shy or silly, to indicate that he was welcome to stay. Instead...

Treating me as if I was a monster.

His own harsh words, only a few hours ago, showing he had not forgotten either.

But once he'd walked away, she thought wretchedly, it had seemed impossible—unthinkable—to call him back. And so much easier to go into denial about everything she felt for him. To pretend that the love—and the need—did not exist. And never would.

A pretence she would now have to sustain for whatever was left of their marriage.

When all I truly want to do is fall on my knees and beg him to love me, she thought, wrapping her arms round her body to stem the tide of desolation that was threatening to overwhelm her.

Because she knew that it was all much too late.

CHAPTER ELEVEN

IT WAS an hour later when Raf returned.

Emily was seated at her dressing table, brushing her hair, when she became aware of a sudden stir, as if the house was waking up to its master's arrival. She heard his voice asking an imperious question and mentally braced herself, knowing that he would come in search of her.

And, only a moment later, he appeared in the doorway behind her and stood leaning against the frame, watching her in silence.

'Oh, hi.' Emily tried for nonchalance. 'Have—have you had a good day?' *Did you meet Valentina? Were you together in your apartment?*

His dark face relaxed into a sudden smile and, in spite of everything, she felt her heart miss a beat. 'It has been interesting, *mia cara*,' he drawled. 'Why do you ask?'

'Isn't that what wives are supposed to ask—when their husbands come home from the office?'

'How would I know?' He gave a faint shrug. 'I have never had a wife before.'

He walked across the room, removing his jacket and tossing it on to the bed, then took the brush from her, putting it aside. His hands descended to her shoulders as the hazel eyes met hers watchfully in the mirror. 'But, as you have asked,' he went on softly, 'I found concentration difficult, because I was thinking about you.'

He bent, letting his lips brush her cheek. 'Tell me, *carissima*, have I been forgiven?'

'For what?' she asked with faint breathlessness.

'For once again forcing you to have sex with me when you did not wish to do so.'

Her hesitation was momentary. She said softly, 'I think we both know that isn't true.' And turned, offering him her mouth.

His kiss was deep and lingering, but when at last he raised his head it was to run a rueful hand round his chin.

'I must not damage your beautiful skin. Come and talk with me while I shave, *carissima*.'

She followed him into the bathroom, clicking her tongue as she rescued his rapidly discarded shirt and tie from the floor on the way.

'You were never so untidy at the cottage.'

He was unrepentant. 'But I had no staff at the cottage to wait on me. Here it is different.'

'And you didn't tell me you could cook.'

'Ah,' he said, 'Fiona has been talking to you. Telling my secrets.' *But none that really matter...*

She sat on the broad tiled rim of the bath as he applied the foam to his face, watching the play of muscle under the smooth skin of his back.

'On the subject of staff,' she said carefully. 'Must I really have a maid?'

'I fear so.' Raf picked up a razor. 'You are going to lead a busy life here, *mia bella*, and you may have to change your clothes several times a day. You need someone to keep your wardrobe in order and advise you on what to wear for your various engagements.' He paused. 'And I understand the girl is well-qualified, with excellent references.'

And looks as if she's permanently sucking a lemon, Emily thought, sighing soundlessly.

'I have also arranged for you to have a personal driver,' he went on, removing the lather with long, expert strokes. 'His name is Stefano, and you will meet him tomorrow.'

Emily gasped. 'Is that strictly necessary?'

'Of course,' he said. 'Or I would not employ him. It is a security measure, *mia bella*.'

She bent her head. 'Wouldn't it be easier and cheaper just to send me home?'

'No,' he said. 'Think what it would cost in time and money

for me to fly to England each time I wished to make love to you.'
He paused. 'And for the present, Emilia, this is your home.'
There was a warning edge to his voice. 'Try to remember that.'

For the present...

'So,' he went on, 'did you like Marcello's Fiona?'

Emily pulled herself back from the edge of sadness. 'Yes, she
was lovely.' Her smile was involuntary. 'It was kind of you to
arrange it.'

'I thought meeting a fellow Briton might make your exile
easier to bear,' he said drily. He cleaned his razor and dried his
face, then walked over to her, lifting her to her feet. 'Thank me,
then,' he whispered.

He bent, rubbing his newly smooth cheek gently against hers,
and she moved closer, pressing herself against him, her lips
already parting for his kiss.

As his mouth caressed hers, his hand sought the swell of her
breast, stroking the nipple with tender expertise, making her
catch her breath in swift, irresistible pleasure.

He murmured her name and pulled her nearer still, his hands
sliding down to her hips, so that her body ground against his. At
the same time, she felt his lips burning on her breast through the
thin wool of her sweater.

But, even as her body responded with its first voluptuous
shiver of desire to the implicit demand of his touch, she heard a
faint sound.

Raf heard it too, freezing instantly, his head turning sharply
towards the open bathroom door, and, as Emily followed his
gaze, she saw Apollonia standing there, holding an armful of
clean towels as she stared at them.

Raf's hands fell away and he said something quiet and violent
under his breath, before striding over to the girl, taking the towels
and dropping them to the floor, then grasping her elbow and
marching her out of the room.

Emily could hear him speaking low furious Italian all the
way across the bedroom until finally its door slammed and he
returned alone, his face still set and angry.

'She goes,' he said flatly. 'As soon as her replacement can be
found.' He paused. 'What was the name you said?'

'Apollonia.' To her own surprise, Emily felt a pang of compunction for the girl whose dream job was over almost before it had begun. 'Raf—isn't that a little hasty? She made a mistake. It—it could have been worse.'

'Why, yes,' he said, with a touch of grimness. 'She could have walked in without knocking five minutes later. And I have no wish to find her standing over us while I am making love to you, Emilia.'

'I think you already made that clear,' she said ruefully. 'But in the past she's worked for old ladies who live alone. Maybe she's not used to—men in bedrooms.'

'Particularly her own, *indubbiamente*,' Raf said sourly.

'That's not very kind,' Emily rebuked him with severity.

'She is hardly decorative,' he said, frowning a little. 'And it seems to me that I have thought that before, although I cannot at present remember when or where.' He slid an arm round her waist. 'Perhaps I shall feel more charitable after dinner.'

They were sipping their *aperitivos* in the *salotto* when Gaspare came in looking glum. Preparations for dinner had completely halted, he announced, because the girl Apollonia was weeping on Rosanna's shoulder.

'She is hysterical.' He spread his hands. 'She fears Your Excellency means to dismiss her.'

'Her fears are justified,' Raf responded curtly. 'However, the Contessa has asked me to think again, so you had better bring her to me.'

Red eyes and a pink nose had done nothing to enhance Apollonia's appearance. When she saw Raf she rushed forward, breaking into an impassioned flood of Italian.

He lifted a hand to check her. 'In English,' he instructed. 'So the Contessa can understand what is being said. You are to be given another chance, Apollonia, but there will not be a third.'

She tried to kiss his hand, but he stepped back out of reach. 'It is my wife you must thank,' he said crisply. 'She spoke for you. But remember this. In future, when the Contessa and I are alone together in our suite, we do not wish to be disturbed. *Capisci*?'

'I—understand,' the girl muttered. She turned to Emily, her expression still sullen. '*Grazie, vossignoria.* I will work hard for you.'

'A look that would scare birds from fields,' Raf commented tersely when the maid had been led away. 'Are you sure you wish to keep her, *mia cara*?'

Emily sipped her Campari. 'She'll mellow,' she said, trying to sound confident. 'And everyone deserves a second chance—don't they?'

'Do they?' Raf turned away, his face suddenly remote as he poured himself another whisky. 'I hope you are right. But somehow I doubt it.' He raised his glass, his mouth twisting cynically. 'To real life,' he said, without looking at her, and drank.

Leaving her to stare at him, feeling oddly chilled, as if an icy wind had just swept through the room. And wondering why.

As the days that followed melded into weeks, Emily found that Raf had not exaggerated about how hectic her life would become.

Everyone, it seemed, wanted to meet the young Contessa Di Salis, and invitations poured in. If Emily had chosen, she could have attended a ball, a reception or a party every evening. Instead, she left it to Raf's discrimination to decide what should be accepted and what politely declined.

She was aware, too, that when she appeared in public with Raf, she was the object of avid speculation. But, as he rarely moved more than a few feet from her side, no one dared voice their curiosity out loud. And he firmly vetoed the requests for interviews from editors of newspapers and glossy magazines.

She was also spared any immediate confrontation with Valentina Colona, having learned from a newspaper report that the lady was in the USA promoting her newest cosmetic range venture.

It would happen eventually but, in the meantime, Emily set herself almost grimly to the task of enjoying herself, but soon discovered it was not that difficult.

Having the right clothes helped, of course. Raf had been true to his word about choosing her initial wardrobe and she was half-ashamed to acknowledge that she'd enjoyed being totally indulged in this way and that his eye for colour and style were exemplary.

But then he'd had a good tutor, she reminded herself painfully, more than once, during their marathon shopping expedition. And at least nothing he'd bought her held the Valentina X label.

The underwear he'd selected for her had surprised her the most, managing to be exquisitely pretty, astonishingly demure and lethally expensive, all at the same time.

For his eyes only, she thought wryly. And not a thong in sight.

Life was progressing smoothly on the domestic front too, and she was learning to handle the day-to-day running of her complicated household, largely, she admitted, through the unstinting goodwill of the staff, who clearly wished her to succeed in her new responsibilities.

With one exception, of course. She still hadn't won over the sullen Apollonia. Although she couldn't openly fault her discretion after that first evening, she still had the strangest feeling sometimes that she and Raf were not entirely alone. That there was the odd footfall, not far away, or the occasional sound of a softly closing door.

Or perhaps she was just being paranoid, she thought. This was an old house, so there were bound to be creaks and small noises.

But the girl's efficiency and skill were undeniable. The first time Emily had attended a formal banquet, Apollonia had dressed her hair high in a loose knot on top of her head, allowing a few graceful tendrils to fall round her face, softening the look.

'Did you like my hair?' Emily had asked Raf rather shyly when they'd returned late that night.

'Very much, *carissima*. Because it means I can do—this.' He'd removed the pins one by one, allowing the scented auburn mass to spill down so that he could bury his face in it, before picking her up in his arms and carrying her to bed.

The occasions she really looked forward to were the long informal dinners at the homes of friends, or their own, filled with wine, laughter and passionate debate about every subject under the sun.

She'd been self-conscious at first, but their acceptance of her seemed total, none of them, by a word or look, indicating they found it strange that they'd only just met her after three years.

Sometimes she wondered what they would say amongst themselves when the divorce was announced and she disappeared permanently back to Britain, but resolutely refused to allow herself to dwell on it.

When it happened, she would face it—somehow, although every day and every night she spent with Raf brought with it the inevitability of eventual heartbreak.

The times with Marcello and his wife were especially relaxed and enjoyable and Emily soon found that Fiona was eager to expand her horizons and involve her more deeply in the city's life.

'You can't sit around all day, waiting for Raf to come home,' she'd told her with mock sternness. 'And you need to be more than a lady who lunches. I'm on this international committee for children's charities with a lot of other ex-pats, and they'd love you to come on board too. Can I tell them you will?'

But Emily had refused quietly, saying she didn't feel ready for such commitment.

A decision that Raf had queried a few days later. 'Fiona is disappointed that you will not help on her *commissione*,' he'd told her. 'She has asked me to talk you round, if that is possible.'

'I don't think so,' she'd returned stiltedly. 'I don't want to start something I may not be here to finish.'

There was a silence, then he'd said, his tone cool and remote, 'As you wish, *mia cara*.' And the subject had not been raised again.

But such awkward moments were few. And the times Emily loved best were those that they spent at home together, whether it was in the evenings when she sat curled up in the curve of his arm, talking or listening to music together, or the weekends where they lazed in bed, eating long, delicious breakfasts, while Raf read the newspapers, muttering furiously over the contents, until, of course, he saw her laughing at him and exacted appropriate retribution, all press reports forgotten.

It was at moments like those that she really felt as if she was his wife, and knew she should ask all the still unanswered questions fermenting in her mind, but she was afraid of spoiling the quiet intimacy of those times—or of revealing that they were only an illusion.

Occasionally, as the days passed, she discovered Raf watching her, an odd intensity in his gaze that almost amounted to sadness, and felt her heart thud uneasily, as if she'd received a silent warning that this was simply an interlude in the scheme of things. And that, soon, the real life he'd spoken of would intervene.

In bed, he was still passionately, intuitively skilful, intent on exploiting to its fullest extent their mutual capacity for pleasure. And Emily no longer pretended, even for a moment, that her ardour did not match his.

When he stops making love to me, she thought one heavenly night, just before she fell sated and drowning into sleep, then I'll know…

Only to find that reality was already hovering, casting its shadow over her fragile happiness.

She was lying on the sofa reading late one afternoon, when Gaspare came into the *salotto* to tell her that Rafaele would not be returning that night.

'He has a deal that must be finalised this evening, *signora*, but negotiations are not going well.' He paused. 'Also there is an early breakfast meeting tomorrow. So it will be more convenient for him to remain in the city.'

Emily scrambled to her feet, throwing her book aside. 'Is he on the line? I'll talk to him.'

'The message was from his secretary, *signora*.'

'Oh, yes. Of course.' She resumed her seat, feeling slightly foolish.

These things happen, she told herself, as she tried to get back into the plot of the thriller she was reading. But she couldn't concentrate.

Instead, she found herself thinking again about the apartment. This place she'd never seen as yet. Although, as it existed, it was the obvious place for him to stay.

Also, she knew there was a major deal going down because he'd told her so only a couple of days before when she'd mentioned he seemed preoccupied.

She was fussing over nothing.

At the same time she wished he'd telephoned himself—had spoken to her. And she'd have said—what? Please come home, however late it is. I miss you.

Which was one step away from the forbidden words, I love you, and therefore not very wise. So things were probably best left as they were.

She ate a solitary meal, with Gaspare being extra solicitous and Rosanna sending up all her favourite dishes.

But there was no comfort for her in the wide empty bed and she spent a miserably restless night without him.

She felt heavy-eyed and at odds with herself the following day, even though she was waiting eagerly for a rapturous reunion when he eventually returned.

But it did not happen. His kiss was almost perfunctory, holding none of its usual promise. And, although he said briefly that the deal had been successfully concluded, his thoughts were clearly still elsewhere.

At the conclusion of dinner he got to his feet. 'I have some work to do, Emilia. You will excuse me?'

'Of course.' Another first, she thought, refusing to be dismayed. Instead, she stole a glance at him under her lashes. 'I might even have an early night.'

'A good idea.' He came round the table to her. Kissed her hand, then her cheek in a gesture that brought a stinging reminder of their first, formal days of marriage. Days that she'd thought were behind them for ever.

He added with slight constraint, 'You look tired, *mia cara*. I will make sure you are not disturbed later.'

Which was the exact opposite of what she'd intended. She felt bewilderment and the beginnings of fear as she watched him walk away.

It was a long time later that she heard him come upstairs. She saw the light under the door of the adjoining room, as she'd done every night of that long-ago and lonely honeymoon. Now, as then, she watched it go out. And heard the ensuing bleak and lasting silence.

She released her held breath in a long shuddering sigh as she realised he was sending her the inevitable message that they'd reached the beginning of the end to their marriage.

And she lay, staring into the impenetrable darkness, too frightened even to cry.

* * *

Emily applied a last coating of mascara to her lashes and sat back, viewing her reflection. Cosmetics were only a fragile mask, she thought. They couldn't completely hide the hollows in her cheeks or the shadows beneath her eyes. The tell-tale signs that would signal her unhappiness to the world.

Although the world probably already knew, she acknowledged wearily. For the last fortnight, she'd been aware of speculative glances following her, whispers that stilled at her approach. Perhaps there was pity too, but she couldn't bear to look too closely.

She rose from her dressing stool and walked across to the bed that she'd now occupied alone for two endless weeks. Her dress was waiting there, a heavy silk sheath in sapphire blue that fitted her like a second skin, its boned strapless bodice cupping her breasts like the petals of a flower. A glamorous, sophisticated gown for an important party at the house of one of Rome's most prominent bankers. A big occasion, and maybe the last one she would attend as Raf's wife.

And she would go looking good. She was determined about that, she thought, as Apollonia made one of her silent appearances from nowhere to assist her into the dress.

Emily felt self-conscious as she slipped off the charming *eau-de-nil* satin robe that had been among the lingerie Raf had bought for her in some different lifetime, standing for a moment in a pair of delicate high-legged briefs, and lace-topped stockings.

She'd grown accustomed to Apollonia's continuing ungraciousness, but she still disliked appearing even semi-nude in front of her.

Although she'd finally grown accustomed to undressing in front of Raf, she thought sadly. Had even learned to enjoy uncovering herself for his pleasure and watching his eyes cloud with desire.

But that, of course, was once upon a time. No longer. Now he simply—stayed away, without offering any excuse or explanation. And she couldn't bring herself to ask, because she already knew the answer.

And it was an additional humiliation to realise that Apollonia, of all people, must know exactly when the Count had ceased to visit his wife's bed. And might even extract a sour triumph from her knowledge.

Which meant that the rest of the household were also aware that, after less than two months, their Contessa's days in Italy were surely numbered. Nothing was said, of course. There wasn't a hint that anything might be amiss.

Unlike the wider world, where, she guessed, it would not be entirely unexpected when the axe publicly fell on this ill-matched marriage.

Their friends, of course, would grieve at the outcome and she would miss them, too. Just for a while, she thought, she'd been allowed a glimpse of the kind of life she'd always dreamed about. Where, alongside her passionate relationship with Raf, there was fun and camaraderie to enjoy, too, in a larger circle.

It would not be easy to return to England and begin another life in isolation.

Apollonia said her usual nothing as she eased the dress over Emily's head and pulled it into place. But fastening the long zip turned into an unexpected struggle and Emily could hear her muttering under her breath.

Well, it can't be because I've put on weight, she thought wearily. Because her appetite had failed completely in the past weeks. Raf rarely dined at home these days and she ate mainly to avoid upsetting Rosanna. But she no longer enjoyed her food. In fact, since she'd been sleeping alone, she'd felt permanently tense, nervous and out of sorts.

She'd begun, too, to refuse invitations on her own account, even excusing herself from engagements with Fiona, simply because she didn't want to face anyone.

However, Raf had insisted that they attend tonight's party together. When she'd protested that she did not feel up to it and would rather remain at home, he had said curtly, 'If you are ill, Emilia, you should see a doctor.' And paused. 'Shall I summon one?'

But I'm not sick, she'd wanted to cry out. If you'd just—*just*—take me in your arms again, I'd be fine. I know it.

Instead, she'd said quietly, 'That won't be necessary. I'll go to the party, if that's what you want.'

He was already waiting for her in the wide reception hall below, devastating in formal evening dress as he stood, staring into space with eyes that seemed to see nothing. And Emily, quietly descending the stairs, saw with a pang how weary he looked. How wretched, and almost defeated.

Darling, she whispered silently. Oh, my love—my love...

For a moment it occurred to her that maybe he wasn't finding her impending banishment as easy to command as he'd supposed. But she knew she was being foolish. Rafaele was as ruthless in his private life as in the business world. And he would do whatever was necessary, just as he always had.

So she fought back her overwhelming, ludicrous impulse to run down the remaining stairs to him, fling her arms around him as she kissed away the sadness from his face. Because any such action would achieve nothing, except to embarrass them both.

And little else mattered now but her pride and her dignity.

At that moment he looked up and saw her walking down to him, her slender body swaying in its dark blue sheath, her bare shoulders glowing like ivory against the rich colour, with her auburn hair drawn back from her face and confined at the nape of her neck by a broad gold clip, ornamented by sapphires. And, for a second, she thought she saw something flicker momentarily in his eyes that might almost have been desire.

But all he said was a coldly formal, 'You look very beautiful tonight, Emilia. The dress is a great success. Shall we go?'

One of the massive bedrooms in the house had been made available for the women to leave their wraps and freshen their make-up.

As Emily turned away from the mirror, the small crowd in front of her parted, the laughter and chatter dying away as a woman came towards her. She was tall and poised, her dark hair rippling round her shoulders, her voluptuous body frankly displayed in a revealing black satin gown. Curved lips smiled, showing perfect teeth.

'Contessa' she said. 'This is a pleasure too long deferred. I am Valentina Colona.' She held out a hand and Emily, dazed, allowed her own fingers to touch it.

Almond shaped eyes, black as sloes, looked her over. The smile did not waver. 'Your gown is charming,' she said, the words musically clear in the listening silence around them. 'But in future you should come to me. I know so well what Rafaele likes.'

'Thank you.' Emily found her own voice from somewhere.

'But you have been away, I think, and perhaps you will find his tastes have changed in your absence.'

And, as she walked across to the door and went out, she heard the gasp that followed her.

'Emilia.' Bianca Vantani, wife of another of Raf's friends, came running after her, white-faced with anger. 'How dare she come here, dregs of the gutter as she is, where she is not invited? Because she has not been, I know it.' She hugged Emily fiercely. 'Let my Giorgio find Rafaele, *cara*. Make him take you home.'

'By no means.' Emily lifted her chin. 'I came to a party, and I intend to enjoy it. Let's find some champagne instead.'

Bianca's eyes were like saucers. 'But is that wise?'

'Infinitely wiser than going home, believe me,' Emily said crisply.

Because I have no home. Just an empty house far away in England.

The party was large and crowded, spreading throughout the palatial rooms on the ground floor, so it was nearly three-quarters of an hour before Raf tracked her down. Emily was in a side room flirting determinedly with a very junior member of the British Embassy staff, when she saw him coming towards her. The young man took one look at the Count's face, realised his luck had changed for the worse and discreetly faded away, as Raf took her glass from her hand.

'How many of these have you had?' he asked harshly.

She lifted her chin defiantly. 'Not nearly enough, *signore*.'

His mouth tightened. 'Get your wrap. We are leaving.'

'But we only just got here,' she protested. 'And there are so many *lovely* people still to meet.'

'They will have to wait for another occasion.' His voice was grim. He paused. 'Emilia, I do not wish to carry you to the door, but I will if I must.'

'You'd make a scene in public?' Emily challenged. She shook her head and wished she hadn't when the room swam a little. 'I don't believe it.'

'No scene. I would explain that the heat of the rooms had

made you feel faint—and I would be believed.' His hand closed on her arm. 'Now come with me.'

Not a word was spoken on the journey back to the house, and Raf's profile was pure granite as he stared out of the car window.

I don't know what you have to be so sore about, Emily addressed him in silent bravado. I think you'll find I'm the injured party here.

Unless you've heard what I said to your Valentina, and you're annoyed about that. But what was I supposed to do—just take it? Think again, *signore*.

Once in the house, she went straight upstairs without even bothering to offer him a formal goodnight. But, by the time she reached her room, her mood had begun to change, hurt and anger giving way to a feeling of defiance.

Is that it? she asked herself. She walks back into our lives and reclaims him and I meekly fade out of the picture? Is that what they think—what they hope?

She began to pace backward and forward, the silk of her gown rustling in the quiet of the room.

I looked good tonight, she thought, swinging round to look at herself in the mirror. Everyone said so, and I don't think that was just a sympathy vote.

Nor can I believe, in spite of everything, that Raf's desire for me is stone dead. That he could want me so badly one night, only to cut me out of his life the next.

I *won't* believe it.

But I've allowed this estrangement between us to happen. I've never challenged him or gone to him of my own accord. Instead, I've been fool enough to let my ridiculous pride stand in the way, when I need him so badly. Not just as my lover, either, but as the husband who teases me and laughs with me. Who smiles when our eyes meet across a room. Who holds me in his arms while I sleep and takes my hand when I'm nervous.

Surely—surely out of all this there must be something left for me.

Dear God, I'd settle for so little. So very little.

If only—only I can make him want me again...

She waited tensely until at last she heard him go into his

room and saw the light come on. Then, taking a deep breath, she walked across to the communicating door and knocked.

He opened it at once, his face drawn and remote in the lamp-light.

'It is late,' he said quietly. 'I thought you were asleep. You need your rest.'

She smiled at him. 'Not much rest if I have to sleep in this dress, *signore*.' She turned her back. 'The zip. Do you mind?'

He was silent for a moment. 'Where is Apollonia?' he asked harshly. 'This is what she is paid for.'

'You barred her at night-time, remember?' She looked at him over her shoulder. 'Please help me, Rafaele.' She tried to smile. 'You never objected before.'

His fingers felt icy against her bare skin and they trembled as he undid the tiny hook, then tugged at the zip. Emily felt it give way at last as the dress fell away from her body, baring her to the waist. Slowly, she pushed the folds of fabric down over her hips to the floor and stepped out of them. Then she turned to face him, lifting her hands to release the jewelled clip at the nape of her neck, allowing her hair to tumble over her shoulders.

She saw a hunger he could not disguise flare suddenly in his eyes as he looked at her half-naked body in its wisps of under-wear and she felt an answering surge of hope deep inside her as she said his name, softly and huskily, and waited for him to reach for her.

Only to see him stepping backwards, away from her, his face and voice expressionless as he said, 'I wish you goodnight, Emilia. Sleep well.'

And then the door closed between them with a kind of terrible finality. Shutting her out before she could speak again. Before she could ask why.

Deliberately inflicting, she realised, stunned, the ultimate in rejection. In humiliation. Letting her know that her body had nothing more to offer him. That everything between them was truly and irrevocably over.

What was it he'd once said to her—what he'd promised? *I swear that there will come a time…when you will desire me as much as I want you now. And then, may God help you.*

That time, it seemed, had come, and the pain of it was an agony that nothing could cure. That she would carry with her always.

Real life, she thought numbly. With no second chance.

And she walked, stumbling, to the bed where once he'd taught her such exquisite delight and lay there like a stone as the shocked and hopeless tears poured down her stricken face at last.

CHAPTER TWELVE

AT SOME point, Emily fell asleep, but woke around dawn, shivering and nauseous. She dragged herself from the bed and ran to the bathroom, where she was achingly, horribly sick.

So much for champagne, she thought, leaning back against the tiled wall and waiting for the world to steady itself. But she couldn't blame the champagne for everything that was wrong in her life. Nor could she say she'd been drunk when she'd committed the appalling folly of stripping in front of a man who didn't want her.

I knew exactly what I was doing, she told herself wearily, rinsing her face with cold water. I gambled and I lost. Now I have to live with the shame of it. If that's possible.

She felt her stomach lurch again and groaned silently. Perhaps her symptoms had nothing to do with champagne. Maybe they'd been induced by the misery of having her worst fears confirmed. Of being forced to come to terms with the hell of loneliness that awaited her.

She closed her eyes. Had she really been stupid enough to think that loving him might be enough? she wondered despairingly. That her need might somehow reach out to him and draw him closer? Make him love her in return?

If so, she knew better now. And he had never pretended there would be any permanency in their relationship—not from the first.

And if she'd simply accepted his request for a divorce when it had been made, she would not be facing this intensity of heartbreak now.

But then she would never have tasted the complete fulfilment of passion either. Would never have known what it was to lose herself totally to a man's lips and hands, and the primal driving power of his body sheathed in hers.

Her heart told her with sad honesty that, given the same choice again, she would not change a thing.

That, however badly they were ending, these past six weeks would always be hers to cherish and remember. And no one, not even Valentina Colona with her all her sensual glamour, could take them away from her.

She went back slowly into the bedroom. Soon the house would be waking up and she had no wish to be caught, least of all by Raf, still wearing the wisps of underwear from last night. She discarded them, reaching into a dressing room cupboard for one of the nightgowns that Raf had also chosen for her. It was an exquisite thing, white and filmy, embroidered with tiny silver flowers, but its Empire line style was also intrinsically modest.

At the time, she'd looked at him with a certain irony. 'I thought you didn't approve of nightgowns.'

'They have their uses,' he'd said quietly, after a pause. 'On occasion.'

It was only afterwards that she'd realised, with faint embarrassment, that they were probably intended to signal discreetly those days of the month when her body would not be available to him.

However, what occurred to her now with heart-stopping force was that this was the first time she'd felt the need to put one of them on. And that it had nothing—*nothing at all* to do with her female cycle.

Which seemed, she realised numbly, to have gone into total abeyance.

For a moment she was still, a slender white-clad statue, staring at herself in the mirror with eyes that burned.

Then, slowly, she lifted a hand, pressing it against her abdomen.

No, she thought. *No!* It can't be true. I'm just—late, that's all. And, because of everything else that's been happening in my life, I—I simply didn't realise how time was passing.

I've never been that regular, anyway, she reminded herself,

swallowing. And stress can play havoc with your system. Everyone knows that.

Besides we—he's always been so careful...

Except once, she thought, drawing a sharp uneven breath. That day at the cottage when she'd gone into his arms, for the first time giving herself to him totally and without reserve. When nothing had mattered to either of them but the passionate joining of their bodies and its fulfilment.

Just that once...

She went back into the other room and climbed into bed, pulling the covers over her trembling body until she was almost buried in their shelter. Whispering *'It can't be true'* over and over again as she hid her face in the comfort of the pillow. Knowing, at the same time, that it could be true and probably was.

And wondering how she could tell him. What she could possibly say when he'd made it abundantly clear that she had no further part to play in his life. Knowing that this was the last thing he could ever have intended.

A harsh sob broke from her and she crushed a fist fiercely against her mouth. She couldn't afford to make a sound in case it somehow attracted his attention. Because, in practical terms, only the wooden panels of a door lay between them. In every other way they were divided by an abyss as wide and deep as the Grand Canyon.

And she couldn't face him—not yet. She needed to be alone to think.

To decide, somehow, what to do.

And, at that very moment, she heard a faint creak and realised, dismayed, that the communicating door was, in fact, opening.

Oh, God, she thought, he must have heard me after all.

She closed her eyes and lay still, forcing herself to breathe deeply and evenly. But at the same time she was fully aware of his approach across the room.

Knew when he paused beside the bed. Could feel his eyes looking down at her, searching for her under the shrouding covers.

He said her name softly, but she made no response, not even the flutter of an eyelash, maintaining her breathing, carrying on the pretence, and eventually she heard him sigh, then retreat back the way he had come.

Later, when she was sure he'd left for the day, she dozed a little again and was eventually woken by Apollonia's voice saying, 'Your breakfast, *signora*.'

She struggled upright, pushing her hair back from her face, biting her lip as the smell of the coffee reached her, reviving her nausea.

She said, 'Take it away, please. I'm not hungry. Just draw my bath, please, Apollonia.'

The girl shrugged with her usual indifference, but for a second her eyes were alive with curiosity and malice and Emily found herself almost shrinking away.

I don't like her, she thought. And I was a fool to let her stay.

But Apollonia was the least of her concerns. When Emily arrived downstairs, she found a stack of messages awaiting her. Fiona and Bianca had both rung twice, but Emily didn't have the energy to return their calls. Besides, they'd be wanting to make sure she'd survived last night's encounter with Valentina Colona, and there was no assurance she could give about that.

In fact, there was nothing much she could say at all, she thought. Nothing that would not be some form of self-betrayal.

She told Gaspare that her late night had left her with a headache and she was going to rest quietly in the *salotto* for the rest of the morning.

His face was all concern. 'May I fetch you something for the pain, my lady?' he asked in his careful English.

She forced a smile. 'No, thank you, Gaspare.' *The analgesic to cure the way I hurt hasn't been invented yet.* 'I think sleep is the best thing.'

He nodded. 'I will make sure the staff keep to the other end of the house, my lady. You will not be disturbed.' He gave her a look of commiseration and departed.

I must look as hellish as I feel, Emily thought wryly, as she stretched out on the sofa. She certainly wasn't intending to sleep. She needed to confront her problems, but she soon found her own weariness coupled with the dancing flames in the fireplace were having a soporific effect.

Perhaps when she woke up her mind would be clearer.

But, when she did sleep, she found no rest. Instead, she was tormented by the mass of small unhappy images chasing endlessly through her brain. And knowing that they were only dreams made them no easier to bear. Especially when the face that swam in and out of her consciousness was a woman's. A beautiful face with slanting dark eyes and full lips curved in triumph. A husky voice saying 'Contessa!'—and making it sound like a taunt.

A face and a voice that she needed to escape, she thought, coming back to herself with a sudden start.

Only to find, horrified, that there was no refuge from this particular nightmare. That, incredibly, it was right there in the room with her. Valentina Colona, resplendent in a dark red suit, her mouth and nails coloured to match, long, shapely legs negligently crossed as she sat on the sofa opposite.

'So you are awake at last,' she said. 'But at least you do not snore, which Rafaele must have found a mercy.'

Emily stared at her, lips parting in shocked disbelief. When she spoke, she did not recognise her own voice. 'What the hell are you doing here?'

'I felt it was time we talked, Contessa.' Signora Colona settled herself more comfortably against her cushions. 'A little, very private chat—woman to woman. There are things that need to be said, and, like most men, Rafaele hates scenes. So—I have come to speak for him.'

'I don't think so.' Emily got to her feet. 'I don't know how you got in here, but I'd like you to leave—now.'

'I came in through a door.' The older woman sounded bored. 'Some of your staff, Contessa, recognise who will be the real authority in this house before long.

'Not that I plan to live here,' she added, looking round, her expression disparaging. 'Rafaele has done his best to make it more acceptable to me, but it is still too old—too depressing. I prefer the city, and I shall get my way.'

She looked back at Emily. 'Sit down, Contessa, and try to relax. That is what women in your condition should do, I understand.'

'My condition?' Emily managed. 'What do you mean?'

Valentina Colona sighed irritably. 'I mean that you are carrying Rafaele's child. Do not try to deny it.'

Emily said numbly, 'Did—he tell you that?'

'It was hardly something he could keep from me.' She shrugged. 'I, of course, cannot have children, which has been a great sadness to us both. But you have solved our problem.' She smiled brilliantly. 'Give Rafaele the heir he needs, my dear Emilia—that is what he calls you, is it not?—and I assure you that you will find him more than grateful.'

She paused. 'In fact, I see no reason why you should not continue to live here when the baby is born. It could, *alla fine*, become part of the divorce settlement. Although that is for the future, *naturalmente*, once I am free to remarry. Which will not be soon, as my husband's health has improved.

'But I know that Rafaele will wish you to have every comfort. Also, as his son's mother, you will always be treated with respect. By us both.'

Comfort? thought Emily, anguish tearing at her. Respect? When I know I'll never again sit on the edge of the bath and talk to him while he's shaving—never feel him take my hand in his before we enter a room—never sleep with his lips against my hair. When he's with—*you*!

Aloud, she said, coldly and clearly, 'And if it's a daughter?'

Signora Colona examined her immaculate nails. 'That is not an insuperable difficulty. You are young and healthy, after all, and you do not find Rafaele's attentions disagreeable. Some—accommodation could be reached, I am sure. The perfect answer if there is a difficulty.'

Emily drew a sharp breath. 'You disgust me,' she said thickly.

Another elegant shrug. 'But Rafaele clearly does not, which is all that matters in sex.'

'All that matters?' Emily echoed with contempt. 'And you're supposed to love him?'

'But how conventional you are,' the other woman drawled. 'No wonder you bored him so quickly.' She smiled lazily. 'It is not the first time I have shared him, you little fool, and it will not be the last.

'He likes variety in his bed, as I do myself, and he is attractive—and very rich, so we suit each other well.

'But forget any romantic dreams, my little Contessa. He does not understand—love—as you mean the word. He never has. He cares only about pleasure, which is why he is so fascinating as a lover.'

Her smile widened. 'However, I hope you have not allowed yourself to fall in love with him, *cara*. It would only embarrass him.

'And I forgive you last night's little jibe,' she added softly. 'Because I knew, even as you spoke, that you were deluding yourself. That Rafaele has tastes that your bourgeois naïveté could never comprehend, or satisfy. But that I can.'

She rose to her feet. 'Please believe that I have spoken only for your good, and to explain the situation that now exists.' She sounded almost casual. 'I hope we understand each other better and that, in time, we may become friends.'

Emily lifted her chin. 'And please believe, in turn, that I would as soon make friends with a rattlesnake.'

Valentina Colona took a step towards her. 'You are being stupid,' she said softly as Emily instinctively recoiled. 'Now, take my warning. Adapt—accept and you will survive. Fight, and you will lose everything, including your right to your child. Rafaele is irritated by opposition and he can be ruthless.'

She smiled again, this time almost blandly. 'And now I must take my leave.' She walked across to the tall glass doors that led to the terrace and paused. '*Arrivederci*, Contessa. I am sure we shall meet again soon. And I wish you good health. I am told these early weeks of pregnancy can be so very trying.'

Emily watched the door open, then close again. Saw the dark red suit crossing the terrace and disappearing into the grounds beyond.

Then her legs gave way and she sank down on to her knees and stayed there for a long time, staring blindly into space. Listening to the desperate, desolate thudding of her heart. Beyond tears, beyond hope.

Simply thinking—thinking…

Until, at last, she knew what she had to do. And how to do it. White-faced but composed, she rang the bell. 'Gaspare,' she said, when he appeared. 'Will you tell Stefano to bring the car round in ten minutes, please?' She paused. 'My headache's better now and I'm going into the city to have lunch with Signora Albero.' And hated herself for lying.

'Emily, my dear.' Leonard Henshaw rose to greet her as she was shown into his panelled office. 'What a delightful surprise. When I spoke to Rafaele three days ago, he didn't tell me you were planning a visit.'

Because he didn't know, thought Emily. Not when she'd simply walked out of his house, with a change of underwear and her passport stuffed into her largest handbag. She hadn't even left a note. There was no need, when Valentina Colona would be delighted to explain everything to him.

And while the ever-patient Stefano had settled down with his newspaper to wait at the front of her favourite restaurant, she'd marched straight through to its rear door and out into the cool spring day. It was a dirty trick to play on someone she'd grown to like, but she'd told herself she had no choice. She didn't have much ready cash, either, but there'd been enough to get her a cab to the airport.

She'd brought with her, too, the credit card Raf had given her with its astronomical upper limit, using it for the first and last time to buy herself a first class air ticket to Britain, courtesy of a cancellation.

Now she smiled at Mr Henshaw, brighter than bright. 'It's rather more than a visit. I've come back here to live. At the Manor.' She paused. 'As you know, it's my birthday soon and the trust will end. I really need to know the level of income I can expect from the money my father left, so that I can make proper plans for the future.'

'Plans?' Mr Henshaw's jaw dropped. 'But my dear child—your husband—Rafaele. He must have spoken to you.'

Emily looked down at her bare hands. Thought suddenly of lean brown fingers intertwined with hers. Fought once again for control, and won.

Just.

She said quietly, 'The Count Di Salis and I have parted. For good this time. And please don't look so unhappy for me,' she added swiftly. 'At least I have my own home and my own money. Everything will be fine.'

'My dear girl.' Mr Henshaw was visibly agitated. 'This is terrible. Rafaele was supposed to tell you—to explain.'

Emily lifted her chin. 'I find I don't care for the Count's explanations—about anything. If there's something I should know, I'd rather hear it from you.'

Leonard Henshaw rose and walked over to the window.

'Your father had no money.' His tone was heavy. 'In the two years before his death he invested in unwise speculative ventures, looking for quick profits. But none of them prospered and he lost almost everything he had. Even your husband could only retrieve a little on his behalf from the ensuing mess.'

Emily stared at him. 'But the trust...'

'Established with your husband's money at the time of your marriage.'

'I want nothing from him,' she said curtly. 'If there's no other way, I'll—sell the Manor.'

He gestured almost helplessly. 'My dear—your father remortgaged the property for far more than it was worth to finance his business deals. Your husband repaid the loans and, as a consequence, Sir Travers made the Manor over to him.'

'So I have nothing,' she said flatly. 'Why wasn't I warned?'

'Your father was a proud man, my dear. Nothing could be said in his lifetime. And, as Rafaele's wife, what was his would naturally become yours too.'

'Rafaele,' she said wildly. 'Oh, God, why didn't he simply pay my father what he owed him and let us keep our home? Couldn't he have done that? Did he have to take everything from me?'

Mr Henshaw gave her an austere look. 'Your husband has been generosity itself. And he never owed money to your father,' he added. 'It was a different kind of debt.'

'I don't understand.'

'Some years ago, when Rafaele Di Salis was just starting out in the financial world, he was offered what seemed the deal of a lifetime,' he told her quietly. 'He would have become a billionaire before he was twenty five. Only a man—someone he'd met only once—came to him as a friend, warned him quietly that things were not as they seemed. That his potential partners were taking advantage of his inexperience and were involved in a scam that could destroy him. That he could even go to jail.'

He paused. 'That man was your father. And the Count never forgot the good advice that had saved him from disaster. So when Sir Travers was in difficulties, he came immediately to his aid. The only one who did,' he added with some bitterness.

There was a silence, then Emily said jerkily, 'I—see. I only wish that his offer of assistance hadn't involved me.'

'And I'm sorry that you feel like that, my dear.' Mr Henshaw looked at her sadly. 'I have always found your husband's conduct admirable.'

She managed a shadow of a smile. 'But then, Mr Henshaw, you're not a woman.'

Her mind was reeling as she drove back to the Manor—the house she'd always thought of as her ultimate sanctuary, until an hour ago.

And Raf hadn't said a word. He'd let her go on thinking that, once she was twenty-one, freedom and independence would be hers for the taking.

Yet here she was, with hardly more than the clothes she stood up in. Untrained for anything, homeless and pregnant. Also, if she was honest, scared. And—lonely.

But she wouldn't let herself think like that. She couldn't afford to. She had to make a life for herself where she was no longer dependent on or answerable to anyone.

After all, as Valentina Colona had reminded her, she was young and healthy. She could cope.

Just as long as she didn't allow herself to look back—to remember...

The house received her quietly. She dropped her bag on to the hall table, calling, 'Penny dear, I'm—back.' Reminding herself that she could no longer say, I'm home.

There was no answer and she shrugged and walked into the drawing room. Then checked, her hand going to her mouth.

Because Raf was standing by the window, tall and dark

against the thin sunlight. Unmoving and silent as he looked at her across the endless space of the room. Waiting—for her.

Eventually, she said unevenly, 'If you've come to tell me this is your house—you're too late. I already know. And I'll be moving out as soon as possible.'

'No,' he said. 'That is not why I am here.'

'I thought—if we spoke—it would be through our lawyers.'

'If we spoke?' he repeated almost wonderingly. 'You leave without a word to anyone—least of all myself. When the first I know of your departure is Stefano contacting me, weeping, convinced that you have been kidnapped. When I find my servants, who adore you, distraught, asking if they are to blame for your absence.

'When I discover there was no rendezvous with Fiona. That she too has heard nothing.'

His voice rose harshly. 'And you thought, did you, *mia sposa*, that I would simply accept your desertion?'

'You don't have a choice,' she said. 'I've left you, *signore*, and I'm not coming back. But you don't have to worry. I want nothing from you. I intend to get a job and somewhere to live, and I'll do it on my own.'

He moved forward and Emily saw him clearly for the first time. He was haggard and unshaven and his eyes looked raw.

For one helpless moment, her heart twisted inside her.

He said, 'How simple you make it sound—your decision to deprive me at one blow of both my wife and my unborn child. But finding work is not easy without qualifications.'

'But I'll manage,' she said. 'If all else fails, I can always put my training at your hands to good use and become a high class hooker. Maybe I can even ask you for a reference.'

He gasped and she saw the blood blaze into his face. Saw the anger in his eyes as he took a step towards her.

She recoiled instantly, her hands going up as if to ward him off, but in an instant he had himself under control again, turning back to look out of the window.

He said slowly, 'My mother died when I was born, Emilia. One of those tragic mischances that no one can foresee, but which my father, who adored her, was never able to accept.'

He flung back his head. 'And because of that he never truly accepted me either.'

Emily said, 'Raf...' but he shook his head.

'Let me finish. I need, even as things are between us, to tell you this. For him, the world stopped on the day he lost her. And, some years later, when he neglected a chill he'd caught out hunting and it turned to pneumonia, he did not even try to fight for his life.

'I swore then, as a boy, that I would never allow a woman to have such power over me. That I would never care so deeply that I could not walk away.

'And I kept my vow,' he added, his mouth twisting sardonically. 'Until, one day at your father's house, you came flying into his study, and it seemed as if every springtime I had ever known came with you.

'And, for the first time in my life, I understood how my father had felt. What had driven him.'

Emily felt herself begin to tremble. She told herself she couldn't listen to this. That she must stop him—now, but no words would come, and after a moment, Raf went on, his voice quiet and reflective.

'You told me once that you hated me. I hoped—I think I even prayed—that it was not true. I told myself it was impossible that I could love you so much and receive nothing in return. That eventually everything I felt for you must reach you—touch you, and I had only to be patient.

'That there would be a moment in my arms when you would smile at me and whisper, "*Ti amo.* I love you." But you said nothing. Ever. Not even when you knew we had made our first child together. And somehow that was the most hurtful thing of all.'

Emily shook off the spell that had her in its grasp.

'You talk about hurt?' she threw back at him hoarsely. 'You dare mention the word love—when your mistress paid me a visit, apparently at your instigation.' She lifted her chin. 'When she set me straight on the future you both had planned for me, and—and the baby. You wonder that I decided I'd rather be alone? That I want nothing more to do with you?'

'If you refer to Valentina Colona, I learned she had been at my house.' His voice was hard. 'It seems your maid, Apollonia, admitted her secretly, knowing you were alone.'

He paused. 'I said, if you remember, that I thought I had seen the girl before, and I was right. She had once worked for Valentina. And she was still being paid by her—to report back on every detail of our marriage.'

Her lips parted in shock. 'Apollonia was—spying on us? There were times when I wondered…'

'She confessed everything on the day you left,' he said. 'Rosanna caught her trying to sneak out through a side door with her suitcase while the house was in uproar. She thought it strange, so she locked her in a pantry to await my return.

'Apollonia had taken some of your clothes and a few small items of jewellery, so the threat of prosecution loosened her tongue admirably.

'And Valentina Colona is not my mistress,' he added with cold emphasis. 'We were once briefly involved and I have no defence to offer except that I was alone and unhappy and she made it clear she wanted me. But it was over almost as soon as it began. And it has never been resumed in any way.'

She drew a sharp breath. 'I—I don't believe you.'

'No,' he said bitterly. 'You would, naturally, prefer to put your faith in the lies of a vengeful bitch.'

'Do you deny there were stories in the papers about your plans to marry her?' she challenged.

'*Si*,' he agreed. 'There were stories but solely of her invention. They bore no relation to any plan of mine.'

'Why should she do that?'

He shrugged. 'Because she believes she is irresistible, and clearly I did not agree. Something she could not forgive, so her self-esteem demanded that the record must be adjusted—publicly. Not merely a transient *affaire*,' he added drily, 'but a permanent relationship.'

His mouth twisted. 'She told me at the time that she would make me sorry. I assumed that the lies in the newspapers were as far as she would go. But I was wrong.'

He paused. 'Also, and more importantly, I rejected the opportunity to finance the expansion of her business ventures, after she learned that her husband would invest no more money in Valentina X. And she, with equal determination, has refused to accept my decision.

'Even when we were in Scotland, her company accountants were bombarding me with requests for further meetings, all of which I declined.

'So, according to Apollonia, I had to be punished. And, it seems, she saw the manipulation of my already shaky marriage into breakdown as her ideal revenge. Because I too would undergo public rejection. And by the girl that all Rome knew was carrying my child.'

She swallowed. 'But that's impossible. I didn't know myself—not until the day I left. I was horribly sick when I woke up, so I started doing sums.'

He almost smiled. '*Davvero*? I did my own mathematics several weeks ago. And almost immediately I was tackled by Marcello's mother,' he added drily. 'She told me that she could see it in your face, and that she was never wrong.'

'After that, I found myself being congratulated on all sides over my impending fatherhood.' He paused. 'By everyone, that is, except the girl who would make it a wonderful reality for me.

'Every day I hoped—I waited for you to come to me—to tell me, but you said nothing.' He bent his head. 'And I began to think that your silence meant you were angry. That you did not want our baby, because it would tie you to me and you wished only to be free. And then I began to be angry too.'

She stared at him. 'Is that why you stopped sleeping with me?'

He said quietly, 'A friend of mine is an obstetrician—a good man. I went to him because I had begun to think about my mother, and there were questions I wished to ask.'

Emily's heart missed a beat. 'Did he put your mind at rest?'

'He said it was a rare condition, a one in a million thing, and that these days medical science could deal with it.' He paused. 'But he also said that making love in the early months might harm the baby. That it would be better to wait until your pregnancy was well-established.

'That night I saw how tired you looked and I knew he was right.' His mouth twisted wryly. 'So I decided it would be better to remove myself from temptation altogether by sleeping in another room.'

She said huskily, 'I—I thought you didn't want me...'

'Always—always.' Raf's eyes were anguished as they met hers. 'From that first moment, and for ever.' He took a step towards her, then hesitated. 'Emilia, listen to me, *carissima*. You said you wished to have no more to do with me, and it may be that things have become so wrong between us that there is no way back. But, even if you cannot love me in the way that I long for, I still wish to take care of you, and our child.'

He drew a deep breath. 'If you come back to me—to my protection, I will ask for nothing else. We will live as you decide.'

Her brows lifted. 'You mean—myself at the house and you in your apartment in Rome? You'd agree to that?'

He bowed his head. 'If that is what you wish.'

'I'll tell you what I wish,' she said with sudden fierceness. 'I wish you would take me in your arms and never let me go. Because there's nothing in this world for me without you.

'I wish I'd said "Don't go" on our wedding night, and shown you then how much I wanted you.

'I wish you'd sleep with me tonight and every night for the rest of our lives. And that you'll live with me, and scold me and spoil me and make me laugh. And take care of me and all the babies I hope we'll have.

'And I wish with all my heart that you'll believe me now, my darling, when I say—*ti amo*. I love you—love you... And I always have.'

He came to her, lifting her off her feet and putting her down on to one of the sofas as gently as if she were made of glass. Then he knelt beside her, his face buried against her stomach, and she stroked his hair with tender hands and whispered all the things she had never dared say to him before, and knew that the freedom she'd wanted was hers at last.

When Raf raised his head, there were tears on his face. He said softly,

'Do you believe in miracles, *mi amore*?'

'I believe in us.' She kissed him on the mouth, her lips warm and lingering as they smiled against his. 'And, whatever your doctor friend may say, *mio caro*,' she whispered huskily, 'tonight you will most definitely need to shave. And that's a promise.'

FREE

4 BOOKS AND A SURPRISE GIFT!

We would like to take this opportunity to thank you for reading this Mills & Boon® book by offering you the chance to take FOUR more specially selected titles from the Modern Romance™ series absolutely FREE! We're also making this offer to introduce you to the benefits of the Mills & Boon® Reader Service™—

> ★ FREE home delivery
> ★ FREE gifts and competitions
> ★ FREE monthly Newsletter
> ★ Books available before they're in the shops
> ★ Exclusive Reader Service offers

Accepting these FREE books and gift places you under no obligation to buy; you may cancel at any time, even after receiving your free shipment. Simply complete your details below and return the entire page to the address below. You don't even need a stamp!

YES! Please send me 4 free Modern Romance books and a surprise gift. I understand that unless you hear from me, I will receive 6 superb new titles every month for just £2.80 each, postage and packing free. I am under no obligation to purchase any books and may cancel my subscription at any time. The free books and gift will be mine to keep in any case.

P7ZEE

Ms/Mrs/Miss/Mr...Initials ....

BLOCK CAPITALS PLEASE

Surname ....

Address ....

....

....Postcode ....

Send this whole page to:

The Reader Service, FREEPOST CN81, Croydon, CR9 3WZ